THE INNOCENT BEAVER
FROM BIG BLACK RIVER

by Val Valiquette

Order this book online at www.trafford.com
or email orders@trafford.com

Most Trafford titles are also available at major online book retailers.

© Copyright 2010 Valmore Valiquette.
All rights reserved. No part of this publication may be reproduced, stored in a retrieval system, or transmitted, in any form or by any means, electronic, mechanical, photocopying, recording, or otherwise, without the written prior permission of the author.

Printed in Victoria, BC, Canada.

ISBN: 978-1-4269-2112-4

Our mission is to efficiently provide the world's finest, most comprehensive book publishing service, enabling every author to experience success. To find out how to publish your book, your way, and have it available worldwide, visit us online at www.trafford.com

Trafford rev. 12/11/2009

Trafford PUBLISHING® www.trafford.com

North America & international
toll-free: 1 888 232 4444 (USA & Canada)
phone: 250 383 6864 ♦ fax: 812 355 4082

CHAPTER ONE

When he got out of the service, Paul Pauquette was twenty-five years old. Instead of heading home to New England, he moved with his parents to Riverside, California. His parents went to work in the airplane industry; Paul liked to tinker with automobiles and developed a knack in tuning them up, becoming so good at it that he went to work as a tune-up specialist. For years he kept a car or truck in his parents' backyard to fix up in his spare time. When he was finished with them, they ran quite well; Paul had no trouble selling them and developed quite a bank account. He and Dad put their money together and bought apartments. They were both very handy. Working together, they kept their apartments in tiptop shape and had rented them out consistently.

Paul's reputation as a tune-up specialist followed him wherever he went. He met a guy named John Peterson, who developed a car that was a sleeper. A sleeper is a car that doesn't look like it can go fast, but surprises everyone. John talked Paul into being his tune-up man when he had a drag race he wanted to win. He only dragged for pink slips, which meant the one who lost the race also lost his car. Paul was paid from the sale of the parts or even the whole car, when his friend won. Sometimes he would take some of the parts in trade and use them to repair his cars in his dad's backyard.

Paul didn't bother anyone and didn't want to be bothered. He went to church most Sundays, except when he went skiing, hunting or fishing. He loved the outdoors. He didn't believe in having a lot of friends, only a few good ones. He had been burned a few times by people who called themselves friends, and now he was more selective about who could join his social circle. Of course, if you needed a favor, he wouldn't let you down.

Even though Paul had lots of girlfriends, he was reluctant to marry. He had four brothers who were married and they didn't get along very well with their wives, and they beat their kids when they got out of line. So they fought over kids, sex and money. Some got divorced, remarried, and then it started all over again. He hated arguments and figured it was better for him to stay single. This way he could spend his money as he pleased, came and went as he pleased, and generally did what he wanted.

His current girlfriend's name was Alice Lozon. They met through some mutual friends named Bill and Helen Morgan; Paul met Bill while fishing at a local lake. He had been going with Alice for quite some time now. She was French, and his parents liked that. Lately she has been getting serious about their relationship. She was either playing hard to get or she was playing a game to get him to marry her.

Not feeling he had enough to do, Paul had taken up outdoor sports. Fishing, hunting, camping, skiing. He rebuilt a Chevy pick-up to his liking, had a boat built to his specifications, too. He had them both painted the same two-tone colors and stripes. The pick-up had a modified 350-v8 engine with a standard reworked 3-speed transmission with overdrive. It had speed and gave him terrific gas mileage when he controlled his speed and jerk starts. He had 3 gas tanks, which held 60 gallons of gas combined. At 21 miles per gallon, he could travel about 1,266 miles before having to buy gas. He liked that.

The Innocent Beaver of Big Black River

The truck had a fleet side long bed with a Tonneau cover to keep out the rain, which gave him plenty of room to store and protect what he carried back there. It was rigged to pull his boat. His boat was 16 ft. with a wide beam. It had a V bottom tapering to flat in the back. With the 350-v8 engine and jet drive it could get up and go when he wanted to. He could go in very shallow water when he wanted to, not having a prop to hook on the bottom. He fished mostly for bass .He had a deck covering the whole boat except the back where he had his controls. It also had 2 larges gas tanks that held 25 gallons each. He could fish the large lakes and stay out all week if he wanted to. The covered deck had doors that opened so he could store his supplies and sleep in the large space under there.

Getting back to how he met Alice. Paul was fishing at a local lake. He was standing on the dock watching a young boy casting out in the water. The boy was having a hard time so Paul offered some advice. The boy's name was Marty. He introduced Paul to his dad, whose name was Bill Morgan.

They became immediate friends. Bill invited Paul over to his station wagon for some coffee. It was early, so Paul accepted. They had a picnic bench so they all sat and talked, telling each other who they were and what they did for a living. Paul said he was of French Canadian descent. Born in Boston, he moved to Riverside, California after the war. Not married. Worked at a Chevy dealership as a tune-up mechanic.

Bill was married to Helen, and they had three children. Mark was twelve, Agnes was eleven and the baby was two. Bill spent all the time he could with his kids. He was a local truck driver and worked long hours. They lived close to the lake. Loved to barbeque.

It was getting late so Paul said he should be going. They all said goodbye as the kids piled into the station wagon. Bill sat behind the steering wheel.

"We'll have to get together some time and have a few beers." He turned the key. The engine groaned but didn't start. He pumped the gas and tried again, but it remained inert.

Paul had already turned and was walking away, but he stopped and came back when he heard that familiar noise. He walked back toward the station wagon.

"Open the hood."

Bill said he knew Paul wanted to leave, that he would get it fixed later.

"No, open the hood."

Bill pulled on the button. Paul withdrew a small screwdriver from his shirt pocket. He adjusted the carburetor.

"Now try it."

Bill turned the key, and it started right away.

"How did you do that? It's been giving me a bad time for a while now."

Paul answered, "I think you need a tune up."

"You can do it , I'll pay you. My mechanic charges an arm and a leg and this is what I get." Paul asked for a piece of paper and jotted down some parts for Bill to get.

"Get these and call me," Paul said. He wrote down his phone number. "I'll have to do it at your place, which should be convenient for both of us." They both agreed and went their own ways.

Bill got the parts and called Paul on a Friday night.

"Could you come on Saturday? We'll have a barbecue after we're done."

Paul got the address and drove down on Saturday. Naturally, he didn't wear his good clothes. When he arrived the station wagon was in the driveway. Paul, who didn't mess around, went to the car, opened the hood and set his toolbox close. Zip zap, he had the new plugs in and was working on the distributor. Then new points and the condenser. He poured cleaner in the carburetor and sprayed the outside, then started the engine.

The Innocent Beaver of Big Black River

It ran pretty good. He poured a little water in the carburetor as he revved the engine. Black soot came out the tail pipe so bad that it filled the driveway. Realizing he was making a mess, he shut it down. But it purred like a kitten.

It took forty-five minutes, all told. Bill was standing back out of the way. There was no talking or visiting. Paul gave him the impression that when he had something to do, he didn't think, he just did it. He cleaned everything when he was done. Placed his toolbox in his truck.

"Now, if I can wash up, I'm done."

They entered the house. Paul was introduced to Helen and Alice. Alice was a friend who was teaching Agnes to play piano. After Paul washed up and picked up after himself, he sat and listened to Agnes play her favorite song.

Bill was outside watching the steaks on the barbecue. Paul watched as Bill poured beer on them, telling Paul it was his secret recipe. Alice came out and stood next to Paul by the grill.

"Everything is ready inside," she said.

Paul looked at her, and she at him, and they idly chatted about nothing important.

"Alice works at a clothing shop," Bill said. "If you need anything, I bet she could help you get a good deal on some new clothes."

Paul looked at Bill.

"This is all the clothing I have. I guess she could help me now."

They all laughed.

They had a wonderful day, and when Paul left he asked Alice to walk him back to the Chevy. Upon reaching his truck, he asked her if she would go out on a date with him.

"I'd be glad to," she said, and gave him her address and phone number.

On the drive home, Paul thought about Alice; she was very pleasant, not too shy. She was the kind of person who liked fun, within reason.

She and Paul, it turned out, got along just fine. He was in many ways just how he pictured her the day they met. Paul and Alice went everywhere together: movies, dinner, then to her apartment for the evenings. They made love. They liked drive-in movies, but didn't like the food, so they would bring their own and snacks. Naturally there was a certain amount of privacy when they were cuddled together in the Chevy, but she drew the line about getting intimate; other cars were too close.

She liked Paul's boat, but thought it wasn't comfortable.

"What do you expect, it's a fishing boat?" he'd said when she complained.

Alice didn't care for fishing, so Paul usually went alone or took Bill's son Mark. There was room to sleep two under the front deck if they kept the doors open, and most of what they caught they threw back, even though Paul liked to eat fish. The last date Paul had with Alice, they went to a drive in movie. They sat real close together, hands roaming from one place to another. They kissed long and tenderly, each of them feeling their blood course faster, feel beads of sweat emerging through their skin. Then Alice pushed him away.

"We should slow down and relax, or you could be embarrassed."

When Paul went to hold her again she didn't cooperate.

"What's wrong?"

"I just don't feel like it. Let's watch the movie. I hear it's good and I don't want to miss the important parts."

Paul had gotten himself all worked up and now she was letting him down. He didn't like that. It started working on his mind. Could there be someone else? Could he have done something to displease her? Why would she treat him like this? Was she really going to continue this attitude the rest of the evening?

Then he made up his mind.

"I don't like this movie, anyway. Let's go home," he said.

They drove back to her apartment. He was about to get out of his truck when Alice stopped him.

"Good night Paul. I hope you're not going to be angry with me, but I don't feel like making love this evening."

Paul could act independent, too, he thought. He kissed her on the cheek as he started the engine.

"Good night."

She stepped out the door." You go right home now."

Well, that just takes the cake, Paul thought. She gets me to take her to a movie. She gets me all worked up. Then she says good night. There are two things that come to mind here: she's either playing the marriage-for-sex game, or she's found some one else. He thought for sure she would have at least wished him a happy birthday; he had just turned twenty-eight years old, after all. Well, it had been pretty good while it lasted, anyway.

On his way home he stopped at a phone booth and called Grace. She was glad to hear from him.

"It's been a long time," she said, and told him she could see him in an hour. Paul knew this meant she had a previous engagement.

The next day upon arriving home from work, Bill Morgan was sitting there in his station wagon waiting for Paul. They entered Paul's trailer.

Because of his work, Paul moved around from one location to another, and when he changed from one job to another he would also have to find another place to live, preferably close to the job. Now he had lived in this trailer about two years.

Paul motioned for Bill to sit down on the divan.

"Beer?" he asked his guest.

They talked about one thing or another for a while. Then Bill got down to what he came for: to talk marriage.

"You know, Paul," Bill started, "You should be thinking about settling down, getting married and having some kids of your own."

Paul knew what this was all about now. He knew his last date with Alice had been discussed at Bill's house. He didn't like that. Despite this, Paul laughed.

"I just got a thought, an old joke: a married man only wants his single friends to get married because misery loves company." He looked at Bill. "I'm kidding, of course. You and Helen are the best. And look, as far as Alice and I are concerned, sure, someday we'll probably get married. But for now, it's wait-and-see. I want to make sure that if we do marry, it's going to last. And I want to be the one to make that decision not you or anyone else, if you don't mind."

Bill knew that his bringing up marriage would be a disaster, so he changed the subject and talked instead about how well his car ran, and thanked Paul again.

Paul could hear the change in Bill's tone.

"I know when the girls get together they like to make plans," Paul said, "And when things don't go fast enough for them, they get antsy. But they just have to be patient. If it's going to be, it'll be. And they'll be the first to know. Ok?"

"Just don't wait too long. You don't want to lose her." Bill stood up and started for the door. "Well, I'd better get going. Bye, Paul."

Paul thought about his conversation with Bill. He thought about the last time he talked with Alice. Evidently didn't like the way things between them were going, and started crying. And what was he supposed to do about that? He certainly wasn't going to make any decisions about marrying her just to stop her from crying. So he didn't call her for a while, believing that in time, she would just get over it.

It was around three pm Friday afternoon. Paul got a phone call at work. The caller made it short and sweet.

"Tonight at the same place," the voice on the other line said. Then they hung up.

Paul called Alice at work and asked her if she could be with him tonight. She knew what it was all about because he had done it before.

"I have something else planned," she said. "But I guess I can be available, if you really wanted to see me that bad."

He knew she was stringing him along, but he had no choice.

"Please?"

Finally she agreed to be where he told her to be at the appointed time. Paul asked the service manager at the Chevy dealership if he could have the afternoon off. He only did this once in a while when work was slow. His boss gave him a frown but nodded his approval. All Paul had to do was lock up his toolboxes.

His area was always kept clean including the floor; Paul had trained himself to clean up as he went along rather than waiting to do all the mess work at the end of the day. He found that even working this way he still got more accomplished than the other mechanics. He tried to keep his fellow workers out of his area. They wanted to watch him work. They wanted to talk. Tried to slow him down. And they were always pestering him to borrow his tools, which he took pride in, always keeping them in pristine condition. In an effort to keep them away, he had even put a sign on his toolbox: NO TOOLS LOANED. THIS MEANS YOU. Before, coworkers would just open the drawers to his box, take out the tool they wanted, and ask to borrow it only as they were walking back to their own station. He then would have to go around the shop collecting his unreturned tools. But the sign put a stop to that.

Most of the other mechanics didn't openly show a dislike for Paul, but behind his back they cut him up pretty bad. Paul had a few friends at the dealership, though, who kept him informed about the mutterings passed along about him behind his back. The current rumor going around was that he had something going on after work. No one knew what it was, but it was probably illegal.

Paul ate his lunch at the local restaurant or at his workstation. He never went for a drink with the boys after work; he knew that when he'd had a few drinks his tongue tended to loosen up a bit, and he didn't want anyone knowing his business. He made good money because he worked hard and did a good job, and that was all anyone needed to know. Never got comebacks, cars that have to be worked over because they weren't done right the first time. He was a professional, and that was all that should matter, he thought.

After he cleaned up his workspace for the day, Paul went to the washroom and rinsed his hands and face. He changed his clothes, said goodbye to whoever was there, and left. He drove to a filling station that was owned by a friend of his. Alice was parked in a parking space next to the station. She got into Paul's truck and they headed to a drive-in restaurant.

A pretty girl waitress came to the window of the truck to take their order. She put a tray on the door, clamping it onto the window opening.

"Watch out for the paint," Paul said.

"I wouldn't hurt your paint." The girl giggled and gave what Paul thought was a sexy look before walking back into the restaurant to place their order. The waitress knew who Paul was and what he did. She also knew he was single and would make a good catch. But Paul wasn't there to flirt. He was there to meet with John Peterson, the man with the sleeper car.

Paul had tuned it up for him, and he had gotten the most out of it. Any more work on it and the thing would likely blow up. It was a street machine, made only for drag racing. John had invested a lot of money in making the car run so fast, and it was getting a reputation, which was bad, since it was becoming hard to find anyone to race against. When he did find someone to race with, it was always stiff competition with other souped-up cars.

The Innocent Beaver of Big Black River

They only raced for pink slips. All you had to do is sign your name on that little pink slip, and the car went to the person who got it. Using the cars themselves as the stakes for the race had all started for Paul when his parents bought him a car. Both parents worked and felt bad that they weren't there to pay him more attention. So instead of attention, he got a car.

He needed the car to go to school, but he wanted it to chase girls and have some fun. He would drive it to meet with other kids at the drive-in restaurants so he could join them in bragging about how fast their cars were. To prove themselves, they started drag racing. But the town streets weren't made for this, and soon drag racing became illegal. When you got caught, your car was impounded, and your parents had to pay a big fine and bail you out of jail, which Paul knew the authorities liked, even if the kids' parents didn't.

Paul got started with mechanics when he decided to pick up a car that wasn't running. It was certainly a big investment, but he tinkered with it until he got it where he wanted it. Then he started to race. After a few drag races, everyone else got caught and had to pay fines. But not Paul. He kept himself out of trouble.

When he sold the car, it turned out he made more than he expected, and it was then that he figured there might be good money in fixing cars to sell. So he started looked for cars that weren't too badly beaten up and started turning them out, fixed and ready for sale. He had a good eye for cars kids would like and a knack for transforming wrecks into hot commodities. He gained a solid reputation and was happy to have a steady stream of tune-up work on the side; Paul never turned down tax-free money.

Tonight, he sat in his truck waiting for John Peterson to show up so he could find out where the race was taking place. It was John who picked the time and the place. He was a cleaver person, always had an ace up his sleeve. Paul knew the odds had to be in John's favor or the deal was a no-go. To lose it in a race, well that's what it was for. But he had too much money involved in his machine to have it impounded.

The waitress returned with their food. Staring down at their food, Paul and Alice ate and every once in a while scanned the crowd for their friends.

"Hi, Paul."

Paul turned to see who it was.

"Who are you?"

"Never mind who I am. I've got a message for you." The man ducked to look at Alice through Paul's window. "She's all right." He rested his elbow on the window. "The meet is going to take place at Sepulveda, near the airport."

He whispered the time and even mentioned where there was a pretty good spot to park and watch the whole thing.

This was a first, Paul thought. Usually they all met at the drive-in restaurant, looked at each other's machines, and decided where they were going to race before dispersing in different directions. Something was up, and Paul didn't like it.

When they finished their meal, they called to have the tray removed and were about to leave when an acquaintance named Dick Richards walked up to his truck.

"Well, Paul, it's going to be between a Chevy and a Ford." Richards had done the fine tune on the Ford.

"Are you sure its going to be a Ford?"

Richards looked at him in surprise, then turned and walked away. Paul watched as he went over to the others. Paul could see their excitement even through the closed windows of his Chevy; Richards had let the cat out of the bag. Now they knew that Paul's group knew what car they were running. Now, Paul thought, they probably wondered if they should back out of the race. But it was too late. Wheels were already rolling. To back out now would be a disgrace. Their reputation would be ruined.

Paul also thought about how the information was brought to him. By an unknown. Something must have been up, and they were protecting him. He always took precautions, but this was somehow different. He would have to keep his eye out.

Paul drove back to the filling station, swapped his truck for Alice's car and proceeded to the spot where he was to watch the race. It was at the edge of a residential area. The side of the street he was on had a steep bank, which looked down on an empty, houseless street below. He and Alice had a bird's eye view of everything taking place. At the end of the street, there was the ocean. They had a view of the sunset and could see the boats out in the ocean. It was quite pleasing sitting there taking in the view, and for a moment it felt to Paul more like a romantic date than a chance to spy on a drag race. But Paul's thoughts quickly turned. He knew he could have been thinking about Alice, that up here he should be letting thoughts of anything or anyone else float from his mind on the cool night breeze, but he just couldn't make himself forget about the race about to start below. He had worked for three nights straight fine-tuning that Chevy.

Paul had said to Alice that this race was special, probably the last he would do. Like in all races, he fine-tuned everything. The weight of the car, the size of the tires, he even measured out the exact amount of gas it took to run the race, and not a drop more.

For this race John rented a furniture moving van that would hold the two cars. They would load the Ford and Chevy into the van and drive to the sight. If all was clear, they would run the race, load the cars back into the van, and hope to leave before the police caught wind and arrived.

Paul knew the other team wasn't playing fair.

"It's stripped," He told Alice. "It looks pretty strong on the outside with all the speed equipment on it, but inside the car's got another engine, a Chrysler with a turbo charger."

It would be a miracle if they could pull this one off. John's car was the fastest thing around, but this car came from up North. After a few phone calls to some guys who ran the circuit up there, John and Paul soon realized they should watch out for this guy. He was taking every car he went against. If they won this one, Paul thought, they would have the car and make some real money. That Chrysler was worth big bucks. Paul knew John was counting on his skills as a mechanic, but ultimately John would have to count on his driver.

Now the action was starting up down below. Paul saw the moving van way down the street. They evidently had already unloaded the cars, which drove up to what had been declared the starting line. Further up the street, about a quarter mile away, someone stopped their car and was standing next to it, waiting. So they had a starter and a judge to wave on the winner.

It was going to happen real fast. Both Paul and Alice were looking down at the street below when someone pulled up behind him. Leaving their lights on, the person walked up to the driver's-side door. It was a police officer. Paul recognized him as being a friend of Dick Richards.

So that's why he came up to Paul's truck. He wanted to make sure Paul was in on this. With Paul out of the way, he would be tops. Paul rolled down the window.

"Good evening, officer."

The policeman nodded.

"What are you doing here at this hour?"

"We came up here to see the sights. The sunset was beautiful this evening."

"There are better sights down on Pacific Coast Highway."

"Oh, we thought about that, but we decided to come up here where we could be alone. But now that you're here, I guess we'll leave." Paul heard the engines revving below, and glancing out the window, said, "Oh, look. They must be having a race down there."

Alice got out of the car and walked to the edge of the road to see. The officer and Paul joined her.

"Alice," Paul said. "You better not watch, or you could be arrested for aiding and abetting."

Before the officer could say or do anything, the race was over. When the cars got down to the other end of the street, they both turned right, and in no time they had vanished into the dark. Disappeared. Paul motioned to Alice, and they both walked back to the truck.

The race had gone off as slick as could be. Paul knew the strategy. It was all in the start. The other car was faster, had more power than John's car, but John's driver anticipated this. Their car was going to lose the race unless their driver could fake out the other. When the flag came down for the start, John's driver jumped the car just as the flag arced down. He was always fast off the line. He was in first overdrive, which gave him a long run in first gear. He shifted with lightning speed into second over. If he had been a split second late, the race would have been lost. He had his foot to the floor, giving her all she had. He was pulling his opponent by about three car lengths. He couldn't understand how the other car wasn't just whizzing by him.

When the flag went down, the other driver had gotten anxious and put his foot to the floor; the rear wheels let out a squeal, spinning helplessly without traction or acceleration. He just couldn't catch up. His shift was sloppy, and again he floored it, desperately trying to gain on his opponent, wheels frantically spinning again. He spun the wheels for the whole quarter mile. A great plume of burning rubber smoke blanketed the neighborhood.

It was impressive to see, like watching an explosion from far away. A little scary, but no immediate danger. The officer followed Paul. If he's going to do something he'd better do it fast, Paul thought, or I'm going to leave. After Paul got into the car, the officer put his hand on the frame of the open window.

"So this is why you're up here."

"You can't prove that."

The officer took a different approach.

"I'm a friend of yours, Paul, and I have some advice for you, and if you say I told you I'll deny it. The force knows what's going on, racing for profit and so on, and they're watching all of you. Especially you. Because everyone knows that when there's a race, Paul Pauquette will no doubt be there to see who wins so he can get his cut. They know they don't have enough people to catch the racers, so we have instructions to follow you."

Paul turned and looked at Alice, then back at the cop.

"You gave us the slip tonight, Paul, but we're getting better at this. Trust me. We have an informant. He doesn't always know ahead of time where the races are going to take place, but when he does know, he contacts us with his CB. It won't be long before we get all of you, so be careful."

"Thanks for the tip." Paul started his engine, made a U turn and headed back the way he came, waving at the officer. The officer did the same. He followed Paul for a few streets and turned off.

As Paul drove back to the filling station to pick up his truck he thought it might be better to get out of this arrangement. He had a lot to lose here. But before he did any of that, he had resolved to put the skids under Dick Richards. If he wants to be top dog, Paul thought, well he'll be chasing the other dogs around for a while.

At the station they swapped vehicles. She followed Paul back to the restaurant, and they parked in back. When the waitress approached the car, he ordered pie and coffee and told her to bring his girlfriend the same.

Alice stayed in her car, waiting to see what was going to happen. When she saw her pie and coffee arrive, she knew Paul had some business to talk over. She liked this, knowing Paul used her once in a while as an alibi. It was exciting to watch him manipulate the situation to his benefit. If ever approached, she would plead innocent to any accusations made against her.

A perky waitress delivered his order.

"Why don't you take me on one of your little sight-seeing tours?"

"Honey, keep your self ready." Paul winked. "These things happen real fast."

While Paul was eating his pie, John opened his passenger door and hopped in his truck

"We did it."

"Yup."

"Jake is sure a good driver."

"Sure faked him out. I wonder if they're actually going to give up the car. They must have a fortune in it."

"If they're any kind of sportsmen they will. Anyway, I've already got it. All we need now is the pink and if they don't sign the pink over, we've accomplished the same thing. They won't race around here again."

"Remember, if they don't give it up I still get my commission."

John agreed.

"How did you get the car, though?"

"Easy. After the race, both cars went back into the van. The police drove right by us. Boy, it was close, though, Paul."

Paul took a bite of pie and a sip of coffee. Then he looked back over at John.

"I've got something to tell you. When I was up on the hill I was approached by a cop. It so happened he was a friend of mine."

"Yeah, I saw that. Headlights gave him away. I kept my eye on him. I had it covered. I knew if he left you it meant he knew about the race, and we would have split. We knew he would have had to go back to the highway to get down off the hill. Would've had plenty of time to get away."

"He said the police force was going to get all of us," Paul continued. " He said that they had an informant. Uses his CB. The only one I know of with a rig like that is Dick Richards." Paul took another sip, letting it burn his throat just a little as he swallowed. "Now why would he do a thing like that?"

"Don't you know? He does specialty work on the police pursuit cars."

Paul's eyebrows knit.

"Maybe his team figures if they don't beat us they can eliminate us."

"Anyway, won't be long now 'til we get what we always hoped for," John said. "A drag strip is being built in Gardena. We're going to have to keep our cool, because I hear they're going to eliminate dragging for pinks, but they'll have trophies and cash prizes, which could be better, really. Could get sponsors to help us set up our cars and put up cash. It'd be good advertisement for them. Our group is thinking about forgetting about street drags and going into a real dragster. I'll let you know. In any case you'll always be our tune-up specialist, so keep in touch. Hey, and if we get the pink, you get your check."

"Just send the check and don't play around."

John left, and Alice, who was waiting patiently, came over to the truck.

"What now?"

"We have to talk. I'll follow you to your place."

In case they were still being followed, Paul and Alice made sure to maintain the speed limit all the way back to Alice's. There they sat at the kitchen table, looking at one another. Paul started the conversation.

"Bill came over to my place the other night. It seems that you've been talking to Helen. About me. And it seems that you've all decided that I should marry you, or else I might lose you to someone else.

"Alice we became friends a long time ago. You should know me by now. I'm not the marring kind. But if I do change my mind, you'll be the first to know."

She choked up. Looking at him, her eyes got watery. When she regained her composure, she sniffled back tears. Quietly, she spoke.

"You know I've fallen in love with you. I enjoy every moment I'm with you. I hope someday you'll change your mind. I really hope that day is soon. All I want is for us to have a happily married life together with our children. Be a family and grow old together." Alice sniffled again, then wiped her nose as delicately as she could with her long, dainty fingers. "Please don't wait too long."

He was almost ready to put his arms around her and propose to her right there.

Now wasn't the time for lovemaking, so he got up and started for the door. She followed him. He turned to face her.

"I'm just an old bachelor. I'm going to have to have time to think this over. I don't want to make a commitment when I feel this kind of pressure to choose. Please bear with me. It's just going to take more time."

Alice stared straight into his eyes.

"I will tell you this," Paul said. "I do love you."

She came to him and they hugged and kissed long and hard.

"Please," he said, then turned and left.

As he was driving he thought only about Alice. She's got me now, he said to himself, I have to either commit or let her go.

CHAPTER TWO

When Paul got back to his trailer, he had a stack of mail waiting for him. He decided he would look at his mail after he finished eating dinner. He boiled some potatoes, fried a couple pork chops, heated a can of beans, mashed the potatoes and set the table. He washed his face and hands, sat down and started to eat. He turned on the TV to watch the news. His mail was in a pile on the table so he filed through the letters to see what was there. Bills, bills, bills. But what was this? A letter from his dad. Now why would he write to me instead of calling, Paul thought. He must have had a reason. It must be personal.

Paul finished eating, cleaned the table, washed the dishes, put everything away. He then went in and showered and shaved, and while he showered he thought about his dad's letter. What could be so important that he would write? Maybe he sent money, or some legal documents. Paul was in partnership with his dad in purchasing part of an apartment complex. So far, there weren't any problems renting the apartments, and the two of them took care of maintenance; they used the maintenance excuse to inspect the apartments and collect the rent. They had an ironclad agreement with the renters that if the rent wasn't paid on time, the locks would be replaced. They had better control this way and gave better service to the renter.

Paul dried off and put on some sweats; he placed his bills aside and opened his dad's letter.

Hello son.

I got a letter from your Uncle Joe. You know how your uncle travels a lot, and he's always looking up our relations. In this letter he said he was going to visit a cousin who lived in Manitoba, Canada. I haven't seen this cousin for a long, long time. His name is Ed Pauquette. During World War I he left Quebec to avoid being drafted off the streets and forced into the army. That's the way they did it in those days, you know.

Anyway, he traveled the northern lakes and rivers with a Catholic brother from the church, by canoe. They went from one Indian tribe to another preaching and converting the Indians. They ended up at the mouth of a place called Big Black River, on Lake Winnipeg. Joe had been corresponding with him for quite a while and now he's going to see him.

Now, you have to remember that we haven't seen him for many years, and as you know, we're not young anymore. When Joe got the invitation to visit him, he thought of me, which is why he wrote. I would meet him there. It would be like old times, he said, bringing up the past. We would have a lot of laughs and a good time being all together.

I spoke to your mother about her and I going. She said it would be better if I could get you to go along with me, seeing as Joe won't be taking his wife, and your mother didn't want to be the only female there. Instead she said she would stay with your brother Ernest while we're gone.

You're the only one I can count on. You're single, you don't have to worry about a family. Think it over and call or write me back. Or, if you'd rather, come over this weekend and we can talk it over.

                              Dad

Putting the letter down, Paul sat motionless. I'm about due for a vacation, he thought. It would give me some time to decide what I'm going to do about Alice. And there's also the police to worry about. They've got their eyes on me. Things are slow at work. Maybe this would be good for me, after all. I'll quit my job, give up the trailer, and store my tools and stuff over at Dad's while we're gone. Today being Friday, I'll spend the weekend over Dad's so we can make plans.

Aside from the fact that nobody got along, it was a nice family. All Paul's brothers and his sister had children. Lots of them. The bickering and fighting were incessant. Whenever he visited them, he sat in the corner, waiting for the fights to start. And when they did, as they always did, Paul picked up and left. Paul knew there was happiness there, but only when things ran smoothly, which wasn't often enough. The minute problems came up, one had to look out. Better to just get out of the way than end up right in the middle of it.

And they would pester him.

"Why don't you get married?" His family would ask. Or when Paul complained about the fights, they would tell him, "You seem to think you're the expert on people getting along with one another. Maybe you should show us how."

Paul's' answers were always the same.

"I don't need someone to fight with" and, "I don't give lessons. At least not for free."

Today was Saturday. Paul never worked on Saturdays. When he awoke he made his breakfast of ham and eggs, cleaned up his trailer and headed for his parents' home. Upon arriving he noticed his brother Erney's car in the driveway. He wondered if Erney was invited to go on the trip with them. If he was Paul would change his mind about the whole thing. He knew an argument of some sort would erupt within the first five miles of their journey.

Entering the Pauquette house, he said hellos all around. Mom had a cup of coffee waiting for him. She must have seen him drive up. He got a smile from Dad and a gruff nod from Erney. He had expected to sit and talk with Dad, but the conversation never went that way. Paul wasn't sure why this still managed to surprise him. Ernest always controlled the subject, so Paul was forced to wait for an opportunity to interject.

"So I got your letter, Dad—"

"So you're doing it again, huh? Running off with Pa on a wild goose chase. Supposedly to see some long lost cousin with Uncle Joe." He rolled his eyes and huffed.

Erney didn't like the relationship Paul had with his dad. Buying all those apartments, and all of their investments together. Paul asked his dad once why he didn't do more with his other children.

"I don't trust them," he'd said.

Erney knew he wouldn't be going on the trip, so he was trying to put the jinx on it for them. He was always doing things like that. Big and muscular, Ernie never hesitated to push his weight around. Paul used to sit there and take the abuse, but this time when he was accosted by Erney, he stood up and met him straight on.

"What goes on between Dad and I is our business. If he wants to tell you, that's up to him. He asked me to do something for him, which I was reluctant to do. But now, I can't wait. I'll go, Dad, and the sooner the better." He whipped back around to face his brother. "And if you don't like it, too bad. Dad, let's go outside so we can make plans."

They got up and headed for the door with Paul leading the way. Once outside, Paul heard the screen door slam. He saw Erney coming straight at him, hatred in his eyes. Paul faced him, bent a little forward in case Erney rushed him. Seeing this, Erney turned on his heels and went to his car. He spun his tires exiting the driveway, throwing stones all over the place.

"I don't think he said goodbye to Mom."

His father looked at him. "I was wondering how long you were going to take his abuse."

"Dinner's ready," his mother called from the back door. "Where'd your brother go?"

Paul and his father went in and washed up, then sat at the table. All was peace and quiet.

"Sorry about that before," Paul said, eyes wandering over to his mother's. "I'm just not going to take it from him any longer."

All she said was, "I understand."

After dinner, the remaining Pauquettes went into the living room to relax.

"Dad, I think I'll quit my job, give up my trailer and move my tools and belongings here. I don't think my boss will save my job for me when I get back. Probably I'll just get a job somewhere else when I get back, anyway, so giving up the trailer won't be such a big deal. And I can save rent money that way. I'll leave here Sunday after mass, get my stuff out of the trailer. Monday morning I'll quit my job and be back here with my tools and stuff by noon. I'll have the pickup ready to go. So—is it okay if I put my stuff in the garage, at least while we're gone?"

"Sure, son. You know it makes me happy to help."

They sat in silence another minute or two, enjoying the fullness they felt in their stomachs.

The Innocent Beaver of Big Black River

"You and I vacationing together like old times, won't it be something, Paul? But this time it'll be different. We'll be exploring, going into someone else's world. New things to see and do and learn. First of all this cousin married an Indian princess, did you know that?"

Paul shook his head. It hadn't been mentioned in the letter.

"They had four children. Two boys and two girls. I don't know their ages, but I do know one of the boys is about your age. Oh, and a daughter, a bit younger than you, I think. They live at the mouth of Big Black River. Lake Winnipeg. Remember I told you?"

Paul said that he did.

"And Joe said there's a little community up there. Got themselves a fishery, where they clean and pack the fish they catch on the lake. They're sucker whitefish, they catch them with nets. Evidently it's a delicacy, shipped all over the world. It only comes from Lake Winnipeg. They have boats that are twenty, twenty-five feet long, ten to twelve feet wide.

"The fishing is regulated. They make a pretty good living, I hear. They live in small houses built to protect them from the cold. No plumbing, no toilets. Just outhouses and sheds for stowing their things. That's all I know about them, for now. Sounds exciting, eh?"

Paul could see the gleam of excitement in his father's eyes.

"And your truck is in good enough condition to make it up there. Sure glad you decided not to sell it.

"We'll take 395 North, then the 6 through Nevada and Provo, Utah. Then the 89 to Jackson and on to Yellowstone National Park. I'd like to stop there and rest a while, if you don't mind. Then we'll hop on the 212 to 94 East, then the 75 North the rest of the way to Winnipeg. We could leave early Tuesday morning so we can beat the traffic out of town.

"Since you're providing the transportation, I'll buy the gas. But we'll each buy our own food. We go to a place called Selkirk and meet your uncle there. He said he'll be waiting there about a week. I'll send word on ahead that we're on our way, but we've got to make sure we're on time to meet him, 'cause if we don't show you can be sure he'll go on without us."

They went on making their minor to-do lists and finally, figuring they covered mostly everything, gave up for the night and went to bed.

The next morning they went to church. After mass Paul left, heading back to his trailer. He packed all of his belongings in his truck. He had a Tonneau cover for the pick-up bed in the back; it was built so it locked and bolted in place, made it hard to break into. It also kept the rain and dust out. He told his landlord of his plans. The man wasn't pleased, but he wasn't surprised, either. Things like this seemed to happen all the time.

Next morning Paul was at work early, loading his tools and waiting for the service manager to show. He parked his truck outside so there would be no trouble getting out of the service area. As the service manager drove up he saw Paul's truck all loaded up with his tools.

"What's going on?"

Paul never got any customer complaints, or comebacks. In fact, there were customers who requested him personally, refusing to be served by the other mechanics. Because of the workload, some of this work went to other mechanics. When the owners complained they were told Paul was busy and the work had to be given to someone else so as not to hold up the repairs. Certainly they liked the idea of Paul bringing in work, but they weren't quite as keen on the idea that it all had to go to Paul himself. They didn't want him to become a prima donna, so Paul had to take the dirty jobs, which he didn't like.

The service manager also rode him pretty hard. Like usual, he hollered at him across the floor, knowing that Paul was leaving.

"You're not giving me any notice of your intent to leave, and now I'm short-handed."

Paul knew the manager could have taken him into the office, could have done all this in private.

"Well, you wouldn't have given me any notice if you decided to lay me off." Paul didn't miss a beat. "Anyway, work is slow now, and I have something I want to do. It comes first."

"What about comebacks?"

"Have someone else pick 'em up. Remember when I started working here? I did a lot of other people's comebacks. Work that someone else did wrong. And if I remember correctly, some of it I didn't get paid for. You know, as I recall, you were always going to make it up to me—"

"I don't like this. You're going to have a hard time finding another job around here by the time I get done with you."

"I don't need another job. I'm going to start my own garage, across the street. Customers tell me I'm a fool to work in this dump, and I'm thinking I finally ought to take their advice."

Maybe he would do just that when he got back. But for now it was enough to see the look on the service manager's face.

When he was pulling out of the driveway, two mechanics flagged him down.

"Hey, Paul. Heard what you told the boss. Keep us in mind, you know, when you start your shop."

"Sure."

After Paul quit his job, he stopped for gas. Because he did tune-ups for the owner, he had a standing arrangement of two cents off per gallon at this particular station. So naturally, Paul filled his tanks. He also purchased a few quarts of oil for the trip, just in case; that way he wouldn't have to switch brands of oil if something were to happen along the way.

Arriving at his dad's house, Paul backed his truck up to the garage and unloaded it. He already had his air mattress, sleeping bag, camping stove and cooler loaded. As he always did when he went camping, Paul packed his clothes in an army duffel bag.

Nothing for dress. Just the essentials: undergarments, jeans, a good, warm jacket. Then some rain gear and a couple hats.

No one came out of the house, so he took the hidden key and let himself in. His dad's luggage was in a pile near the door, as if waiting for him. Paul hauled all the clothes he wouldn't be needing in Manitoba and put them in his old room, then he went to finish loading the truck.

Paul performed his ritual last-minute check. Extra oil behind the seat. Wiper fluid, break fluid, power steering fluid. He touched his tires. Cool enough to test the pressure. Next the spare. It was bolted tight. He took his thermos and went back into the house. There was hot coffee, and he poured himself a cup. Paul stopped himself. No need to fill the thermos now. He would fill it just before they left in the morning.

Finally his dad arrived, and Paul went out to meet him. He opened the door to the garage so his dad could pull right in. When he got out of the car, he took a few bundles and headed for the truck. While putting the bundles on the seat he turned and on his fingers he counted off.

"Took Mother over Erney's, picked up the rent checks and deposited them in the bank. I told Mother to pick up the rents if we're not back for next month's. Sent a letter to Selkirk, to Joe, should get there in a day or two. Plenty of time to get us there."

Paul was sure he must have at least dozed off for a couple of hours that night, but he couldn't remember. Giving up on getting any more rest, he got up to make all the final preparations for their trip; as he got out of bed, he could hear his father awake, doing the same thing. Acknowledging each other with yawning nods, the two moved silently around the house, locking up. Then they were on their way.

"Let's say a prayer for a good safe trip," Paul's dad said once they had settled in.

Paul kept his eyes on the road.

Looking out the window and then back at his son, the old man reached over and patted Paul on the shoulder.

They traveled right along at sixty miles per hour, even though the limit was fifty-five. They were eating up the miles. The two men sped through Bishop and were climbing over Mammoth when three deer darted across the road. Seeing them in plenty of time, Paul slowed and let them cross the road.

"When you go hunting you don't see them. When you're traveling you have to be careful not to run them over."

Daylight came, and the pair had made it pretty far. Around Provo, Utah they needed gas. Paul pulled into what he thought might be a cut-rate station. He drove up to the attendant.

"Do you give truck rates?"

By the look on the man's face, Paul could tell the answer was no. The attendant stood there holding the nozzle. Paul saluted him and drove to the station across the street.

When they were done they ate at the little dinner next to the station. Tanks and bellies full, they were on their way again. They saw more deer and a couple elk as they approached Yellowstone national Park. From the South Entrance they proceeded to West Thumb camp area where they found a nice camping spot. They were next to a nice old couple. After getting their beds made up Dad went over to visit.

Seeing as their camp area was next to Yellowstone Lake, Paul got out his fishing pole. Being a Federal park, no fishing license was necessary. He caught Dad's eye and motioned that he was going to try his luck. Now the lake near the camp grown was fished out, but there were still some diehards at the shore. Paul walked to the lake, to a spot down the shore where he could be alone. He found a spot next to a large rock formation. Next to the rock formation there was a sandy shore where others had fished before. He tried lures, flies, jigs and worms, but nothing seemed to work. He could see the trout swimming around and they were nice. In order to get them he would have to climb the rock formation, which was about ten feet above the water; then he would lower his hook down to the water.

He couldn't work his bait the way he wanted, so he stood there a minute and sized up the situation. Paul got an idea. He rested his pole against the rock and walked into the woods, turning over some rocks until he found white flies. Carefully, Paul tied one to the end of his hook, then climbed the rock, lowering the fly down into the water. If he cast, Paul figured, the fly would come loose.

No sooner had the fly touched the water he got a strike. He played the fish until it tired, raising the limp fish to the top of the rock. He didn't have anything to hold or carry the fish so he cut a branch from a tree. Cleaning it off, he left a fork about three inches long sticking out. He hooked the fish through the gills and went back to the rock.

In his mind, Paul laughed, telling himself he could have stayed there the rest of the day and caught all the fish. Nah, leave some for someone else, he thought. Be a sport. He picked up his pole and two fish and headed back to the campground. As he was walking by the others at the lakeshore they all turned. Paul imagined they were admiring his catch.

When he reached their camp spot, he showed Dad and the neighbors his fish, He was going to get out his frying pan and stove and start cooking. His neighbor said you were gone only about 1/2 hour. The surprise on everyone's face held a certain reward, in Paul's estimation.

"Well, Paul, one good turn deserves another," Dad said. "Why don't we see if we can't take those fish over to the camp restaurant and see of they won't cook 'em for us?"

When they arrived at the restaurant, they knocked at the door. The cook answered.

"Would you mind cooking these up for us?" Dad asked.

The Innocent Beaver of Big Black River

"Just go around to the front and wait in line. As soon as those guys are done you'll be seated," the cook said, motioning a waitress to take the men to a table.

When the fish arrived on platters, their mouths started to water. Laid before them on both platters were two of the most beautiful trout cooked to perfection, laid out with all the trimmings. It was a sight to see, a shame to mess it all up. But they were hungry.

They started eating when they heard people around them trying to order the same as they had. Naturally the waitress explained that they had caught the fish themselves.

One gentleman came over to their table and asked where and how they had caught them.

Paul grinned.

"After I get done eating I'll meet you outside and tell you."

As he left the restaurant, Paul was surprised to find a group of men all waiting to hear his secret. They in turn were surprised to hear how easy Paul purported it to be. And as he and his father walked back to their camp, a bottle of whiskey shared between them, Paul could not help but let his mind wander to the imagined sight of all those fisherman down by the shore, trusting and relying on his very own trick.

Around three o'clock in the morning, Paul was awakened by something rubbing up against the truck. Usually other campers don't bother you, Paul thought, but maybe someone was trying to break in. He took his flashlight and flashed it around. There in the opening between the Tonneau cover and the truck was the face of a big black bear. With one quick motion he hit the stick that held up the cover, letting it crash down over them with a bang. There was a handle on the inside, and Paul was hanging on as tight as he could. The noise awoke Dad with a start.

"What was that?"

"There's a bear out there." Later, when relaying this story, Paul would remark it was a good thing that when made the Tonneau, he made it out of three-quarter-inch plywood, with laminated fiberglass and epoxy paint, because that made it slippery. Paul and Dad were left to listen to the sound of the bear's claws dragging down the sides of the cover as it slipped on the slick epoxy finish, which Paul would note again was applied by none other than himself.

After about twenty minutes, the pair could hear what sounded like pots and pans being clanged against one another. Soon this silenced the sound of the bear. In fact, if Paul had to guess, he would venture that the bear was gone.

"You can come on out."

Paul lifted the cover and with his flashlight looked around.

"You can take that light out of my eyes now." Paul lowered the flashlight, and the park ranger came into focus. "That bear makes his rounds every night, emptying the garbage cans." The man cocked his head, squinting at Paul and Dad. "Say, you're the ones who started that rush on the trout. I had to speak to a couple of guys you gave advice to, they were tearing up the whole damn forest." He chuckled. "It is a good idea, though. When I get a chance I'm going to try it myself." The ranger tipped his hat toward Paul. "Have a good night."

Paul propped himself up in the pick-up.

"If you see that bear again, tell him we're sorry, but there just wasn't enough room under here for all three of us."

The ranger laughed, then turned, walking back into the murky night. Paul closed the lid to his Tonneau and lay back down in the truck bed, where Dad had already fallen back to sleep.

The next morning they went back to the restaurant for breakfast. After being shown to their table, they both ordered a short stack of pancakes, eggs and bacon and coffee. while waiting for there order the cook came to their table.

"I heard what happened to you last night. You two sure are lucky, but I can't say I don't feel sorry for the bear. If he comes back here again they'll shoot him, you know. Oh, and speaking of luck, I myself am lucky you both came by here. It's all over camp, your little secret. I had to put on more help just to cook all the fish."

"Good to hear," Paul said as their plates were placed in front of them.

"Word is getting around that the best way to show off your fish is to have me cook it. It makes everyone else lick their chops, watching you eat it. You're good for business."

The two men ate their meals in high spirits. When they finished, they got up. The cook came out from the kitchen.

"Stop by anytime and stay awhile. We'll keep the bears away from you next time, promise."

They returned to their truck, packed up and headed out the Northeast exit towards Silver Gate and drove over Bear Tooth Mountain. Paul and Dad stayed on the same bearing, right through Montana and on to North Dakota before finally crossing the border in Emerson, Manitoba. They drove on through Winnipeg to Selkirk, where they meandered the winding back roads until they found the house where Uncle Joe was staying.

CHAPTER THREE

"Boy am I glad you made it. I got your letter or I would have gone on." Shaking hands and greeting everyone, Joe gave big bear hugs to Paul and Dad, asking about the drive.

"We'll tell you later," Dad said.

Joe hugged both Dad and Paul once more. "Alright, well, you ready? Let's go into the house so I can introduce you to our long lost relations."

Upon entering they were greeted by a middle-aged couple. Uncle Joe introduced them as Rose and Pete Lareau.

"Rose is the daughter of my cousin Ray."

Everyone shook hands; they were then invited to sit at the table for dinner. While eating, Dad took pride in telling stories about the trip there, about all the excitement Paul had stirred at Yellowstone. They all looked at Paul with what he took to be awe, and it made him beam. Rose and Pete wanted to know about Paul and his Dad, and Paul was more than happy to oblige.

After dinner Paul took their gear out of the truck, proud to display his equipment in the foyer. He parked the truck out of the way and so the light would shine on it at night, keeping it safe, then sat down on the front steps of the house and looked up at the stars.

"I see you copied me." It was Uncle Joe, who had approached Paul from inside.

Paul's eyebrows knit.

"I mean all those gas tanks. Where'd you learn that trick?"

Paul shrugged.

"Bet you ask for truck rates, too." Joe continued. "I sometimes go right to the refinery, or the gas depot. Sometimes they pump it in, sometimes they don't. But I tell you what, I make 'em sell me the gas," Joe laughed, "Even if it only comes in fifty-five gallon drums and I have to pump it all myself."

Clouds passed over the moon, dampening the light. Paul leaned forward, putting his head in his hands.

"I know Big Black River is off of Lake Winnipeg, but how far is it and how do we get there?"

"Oh, your Dad didn't tell you? I got a captain—Captain Sinclair—to take us up there. He was nice enough to wait here until you arrived, has a cargo ship and hauls fish up and back on a schedule. Think you'll like it, takes a good part of a day to get there, though."

The cloud passed, and the moon felt like a glare like that from the streetlamps down by the car. Paul blinked hard.

"Beds here are good. Better than sleeping in the back of the truck." He smiled at Joe; as if this were some signal, the two men stood up silently and went inside.

"We should offer to pay." By morning, all the gratitude was starting to shake Paul's nerves.

"Joe said they would be insulted," was all Dad had to offer. Paul was still too groggy to argue about it.

Thinking that there would be no place where they were going, Pete drove with Paul to buy some whisky and gin at the provincial liquor store. At Paul's insistence, Dad gave a bottle to Pete for his trouble, not knowing if it was the right thing to do. Pete just nodded his thanks.

Paul knew he and Rose were really going out of their way. He assumed it was because they were related. They probably wanted to make a good impression. It was nice, knowing they had relations like this. Turning back from the register, Paul jogged back to the back aisle and picked up some fruit for his father, figuring he'd appreciate the treat.

They met Captain Sinclair at the dock. His was a regular cargo ship with no staterooms. It had a galley for cooking, but they only cooked for the crew. Paul, Dad and Joe were told to put their possessions anywhere they wanted on deck; they stacked them in a corner, somewhere they figured was out of the way. The ship was two hundred yards long and one hundred feet wide, by Paul's estimation.

Curious and looking for a means of biding his time, Paul put some of the fruit in his pocket and headed for the Captain's cabin. Not thinking twice, he entered.

He was greeted by Captain Sinclair, who told Paul where to sit, seemingly unfazed by the cavalier interruption. Seamlessly, he began to explain that Selkirk was right on the river, which they followed to get to Lake Winnipeg. It had been dredged so large ships could navigate it. He was asked if he wanted to try steering for a while. It was a challenge Paul couldn't resist, and the Captain was happy to oblige.

"I'll show you where the markers and buoys are and all you have to do is steer towards them. The secret is to know when to start turning."

He showed Paul, then stood just behind his right shoulder, as if chaperoning a child; Paul, in return, was anxious in his desire to impress the man with his ability to steer, to keep the ship on course and away from the shoreline.

"You're doing just fine," Sinclair said, turning for the door. "Be back before we have to make the next turn." Looking down at his watch as though it were a map, he winked at Paul and shut the door behind him.

He knew the captain would only be gone only for a few minutes, but Paul worried nonetheless. It wouldn't be long before they came to the lake's mouth. But it must have been safe, Paul thought. Sinclair wouldn't have let him steer if it wasn't. Now the opening was fast approaching. What to do? When in doubt, go straight. Just keep going straight, he told himself. Knuckles white, he stayed the course, eyes on the horizon.

"You passed the test."

Paul laughed, but it was a worried sort of laugh.

"I was talking to your father, who said you worked as a mechanic. You know, I could use someone with that kind of talent. And you already handle this ship as though you've done it before."

Paul stole a glance at the captain, then fixed his eyes back on the water. The captain chuckled. He gave Paul a reading on the compass.

"Just keep it right there, and we'll be just fine."

"Permission to come aboard, sir." It was Dad. "I didn't know you were steering the ship."

"I only did what I was told," Paul said. "I have a good teacher."

Paul, Sinclair and Dad stayed in the control room for the rest of the trip, telling stories and passing the time. The captain periodically checked the compass to make sure they were following the proper bearing. Paul kept the heading as he was instructed; every once in a while he would look at the shoreline as a guide, a way to judge the distance. This made him comfortable, knowing it was there.

But then, as if by some frightening magic, there was water all around him, with no coast in sight. Paul caught himself wondering what would happen if the ship sank. What direction would he swim to make it to shore? He shuddered, trying to visualize a direction, a bearing, taking into consideration the last time he saw the shore. They hadn't made any change in directions, so the closest shore had to be on their right side. But then what of his Dad? In the confusion of making sure his Dad was with him, he could lose his direction. Well, let's just hope nothing bad happens. He hoped the voyage wouldn't take too much longer. He hoped the others around him didn't sense his worry. It was all Paul could do to not to let them hear his sigh of relief when he saw the shore coming into focus. Everything was going to be all right, after all.

It was a long and monotonous trip. By the end of the day, everyone was tired.

"I'll take it from here," Sinclair said.

He started turning the wheel, maneuvering toward the shore, to an opening that looked like a river. There was a large red building and some smaller houses scattered on a hillside. There was a large dock at the building, and the captain eased the ship up to the dock, like parking a car. There were people waiting on the dock, watching the ship, desperate for anything new or exciting to happen.

Most of the other passengers were of Indian heritage, some of mixed descent, all dressed in a similar fashion. Men wore work boots, bib overalls, plaid shirts, and baseball caps. The women stood in the back, wearing long, flowing dresses. Some had shawls. Having thanked the captain for his generosity in transporting them, Paul's party picked up their gear and headed out.

On the dock they were met by a tall, gray-haired gentleman who shook hands and hugged everyone with vigor. He helped with the gear and luggage. He led the way up a hill to his cabin. There he introduced them to his wife, Mofet, and his daughter, Mary. He explained that his sons, Joseph and Jim, would be along later. Paul stood back, nodding his acquaintance and shaking hands.

He told himself he had come along only because it was a help to Dad, that he was being just along for the ride. The cabin was not welcoming in the way Paul had hoped. It was dark, the windows were small, the ceiling so low he was sure he could touch it. But everything was clean, at least. In the corner was a large table, an icebox, a sink; there was even a wood-burning stove. It wouldn't be so bad. It was cozy, Paul told himself.

Cousin Ray explained that Uncle Joe would stay there while Paul and Dad would bunk at Joseph's house.

Then, at Ray's suggestion, they put down their bags and headed to the fish factory for dinner. There was a kitchen for the workers, and the closest place to grab a bite to eat. Paul knew he was eating as a guest of Ray's, but he didn't know how the system worked, if Ray was paying or if he was some sort of member. Usually Paul would have found the situation uncomfortable had he not been so hungry; but he felt starved, and the food was good, so he didn't care. Food was laid out country-style, with great ceramic bowls being passed around the table, followed by a large pot of coffee, with pie and cake for desert. In their satiation, everyone forgot to speak, too wrapped up in eating everything but the plates.

Finally, having gotten their fill, Cousin Ray motivated the group to get up and go back to the cabin.

"Should we get the plates?" Paul asked Ray.

"No, help's got to do it. Come on, let's go."

This made Paul uneasy; someone should pay for the food, the cleaning. He would have to talk to Dad about it later. For now, he would just go along with it. There was always the possibility that Uncle Joe gave Cousin Ray money in advance for expenses. They hadn't paid for anything at Rose and Pete's, and now this. If Paul was sure of one thing, it was that imposing on relations or friends was never a good idea. As soon as he could, he would pay back his share.

Back at the cabin, they sat at the kitchen table, sipped coffee with a little whisky in it and talked. The conversation was mostly in French. Cousin Ray spoke the language clumsily; he didn't get to speak French very often. Most of the people there spoke either English or the natives' tongue.

Paul sat back and listened, joining in with the laughter. He noticed Mary sitting in a corner, trying hard to control herself but unable to stop the giggles from erupting or the tears from dripping down her cheeks. Cousin Ray was recounting the time when Dad and Uncle Joe's family lived in a duplex in Label, P.Q..

"Mrs. Desmereau lived next door, and she wasn't a very nice lady. Since it was a duplex, it also had a duplex outhouse. Each house had its own door and separate toilet, but underneath it was all one hole. On Joe's side the kids made an ice slide from the back door of the house to the outhouse. Now Mrs. Desermeau should have shoveled or paid someone to shovel a walk for her, but instead she used the walk on Joe's side. Seeing as how she didn't like the slippery walk, one night she spread ashes all over it. The next morning, when the kids came out, they saw their slide was coated with ash, completely ruined. Obviously, they knew who did it.

"So one day after school, Joe stood at the back door and waited for Mrs. Desmereau to use the outhouse. Joe headed for their side of the outhouse, then he took a stick and attached a feather to one end like a wand. He reached in the hole, over to her side and tickled her bottom. She let out a holler, got up and looked in the hole. Not seeing anything, she sat down again. Joe reached in again, only this time he did it a little harder. Now she knew there was something there, so she stuck her whole face down in the hole, and Joe's feather was right there to greet her, covered in poop. She let out a much louder holler this time, trying to wipe away the poop, which made it worse. In a hurry she pulled up her panties with her dress tucked into the back and made a mad dash for he house, screaming all the way. They didn't see her for a few days, and when they did she just stuck her nose up in the air and ignored them."

The Innocent Beaver of Big Black River

The cabin filled with laughter, after which things got silent for a while, everyone trying to come up with their own humorous anecdote. Ray piped up again.

"Before I left for the north I heard something about a problem your father had with a farmer who raised pigs. Right, Joe?"

Joe leaned forward in his chair.

"Yeah. One Saturday my father went to this farmer who had some pigs that were ready to butcher. They were enormous, about two hundred pounds. Three of them. My father said he would take them all, provided it was the same price as the last time. Knowing my dad needed the pigs, the farmer raised the price. He knew our family needed the pigs to feed the people who stayed at the boarding house we ran.

So my father says to the guy, 'Look, I've been buying pigs from you for a long time for a fair price. Why the sudden change?'

'Well, Mr. Pauquette,' he says, 'everyone knows my pigs are the best in the area. They also know that whoever gets my pigs gets the railroad boarders. some one else asked for them, but I told them you were first in line. So now, if you want them, you have to pay my price.'

"There were no other pigs close by ready to butcher, so my father agreed. He said he would be by Sunday after church to pick them up. My father knew the farmer went to the ten o'clock mass on Sunday so he went by the farmers place around ten fifteen and poured a bottle of whisky in the pig's trough.

"In the afternoon he went back and pulled up to the pig pen with his wagon. He was ready to pick up the pigs, but they were laying around, drunk as can be. He knew this would happen, so he stood there looking down at the pigs, shaking his head. They were not making a sound.

'Your pigs look kind of sick,' he says.

"The farmer put up his hands. 'They were fine yesterday.' They stood there looking at the pigs for a while. My father said to the farmer. 'I tell you what I'll do. I'll take the pigs at my price, and you don't have to tell anyone, and neither will I.' Reluctantly, the farmer agreed.

"Of course, word spread quickly anyway, and the next morning some boarders approached my father and accused him of feeding them rotten meat. My father said he already butchered one of the pigs but they were welcome to look at the other two. They all congregated at my father's pen. The two pigs were just as spry and healthy as could be. They asked why, then the pigs looked sick before. My father explained that the pigs were just drunk. When word got back to the farmer he was furious, and all my father told him was that he paid him a fair price for his pigs, but from now on he was going to raise his own."

They all laughed. Cousin Ray turned and looked at Paul.

"Do you understand French?"

Paul nodded.

"Your dad tells me you like to hunt and fish, is that right?"

"Yeah. There are a lot of deer, bear and elk around California. We do it mostly for sport, and to get a trophy once in a while." He chuckled.

"You have to be single to do that kind of thing. No woman will put up with you being gone and out of work all the time."

Paul thought about Alice; was she the kind of woman who would mind? He hadn't thought she would be. Actually, he hadn't thought about it much at all. Come to think of it, Paul hadn't noticed many bachelors on his trip so far. Maybe it was this strange, new place. People thought differently about things in this part of the world. From the corner of his eye, he noticed Mary was listening intently, silently. He shrugged it off. Best not to get involved.

Mary sat in one corner and Ray's wife, Mofet, sat in the other. Neither one spoke. There was a tap at the door as it opened, two men entering the already crowded cabin. They looked fit, like they did hard work. Ray rose from his chair and smiled.

"These are my sons, Joseph and Jim," he said, turning to the group. They shook hands all around, then sat and entered into the conversation.

"We were out fishing," said Joseph, "but our catch wasn't very good. End of the season."

"We usually sell them to the factory where they clean them, pack them, and ship them out on Captain Sinclair's steamer," Jim added. "They're a delicacy, you know. End up on kitchen tables all over the world."

They stopped to listen to the conversation at the table, where Dad was answering Ray's question about what happened with the railroad.

"As you know, they were building the railroad North from Montreal. They got as far as our town and were going along all right. And of course we all watched, seeing as how there was nothing else to do at that time. We would sit up on the bank, bragging about how we could build it better, even though we were just kids. They had teams of horses pulling wagons with ties and track and other equipment. The train backed up the track as it was laid. They had a lot of men to do this work. Up ahead they had horses pulling graders where the ties were being laid. It was a slow process. We knew what work was like, having worked hard on the farm. We knew a good team of horses when we saw one.

"I think it was Joe who started it. He called down to the workers and told them they were working too slowly, that they could do better. At first the workers ignored him, but the rest of us joined in and were hassling them pretty bad. Finally, they got fed up with us and chased us off the hill, hollering at us not to come back or else. At the dinner table that evening we told our father what happened. We knew that he left home when he was thirteen, went to the United States and worked on the transcontinental railroad. He started as a water boy and worked his way up to laying track. They had hard times because they had to also fight off the Indians who attacked them."

At this Paul shifted in his seat, looking at his cousins, watching for a reaction. Dad continued.

"When the railroad was finished he got with his last pay a piece of paper, which he kept, not knowing what it was. He only knew that when they gave it to him they told him that it was very important. When he got home he showed the letter to his parents. Of course, it was in English, and no one could read anything but French, so they found an American tourist in town who could translate, and he told them that it was a document stating that he was now a citizen of the United States, if he wanted to be one. And that's why we were all born in the States.

"Anyway, though, he agreed with us that it was taking way to long for them to do the work. That night we figured we would get even for being run off the hill. We went back to the tool shed and busted in and threw most of their tools into a barrel of melted tar, turned the tracks end per end that weren't yet riveted down so the holes wouldn't line up when the workers returned in the morning. unless they turned them back the other way. There were about 10 tracks laying all over the place. You know these tracks were about 18 feet long. They were not as heavy as the tracks of today but they took 10 men and a boy with those pincer bars to lift one.

"When he foreman came in the next day, he knew we did it. He came to our house and confronted our parents. We denied everything. But then he said we must have had help, and that's when we spoke up. We admitted we did it all ourselves, told him we could prove it. That Hector Decorie could lift one by himself.

"When the crew saw us coming they picked up sticks to paddle us with. The foreman told them he was taking care of this, to stand back out of the way.

'All right, let me see you lift one of these tracks,' he says. Four of us spaced ourselves at the track and without hooks lifted it onto the ties and set it down. Then Hector went to the end of the track and bent to lift it and the crew all laughed, thinking he was making fun. He picked it up and threw it off, onto the side of the construction zone. He was one strong young man, and it surprised them, so much that all they could think to do was congratulate him and pat him on the back.

'This doesn't change a thing, though,' said the foreman. 'Damage was done and someone has to pay for it.'

"Now, my father was standing back, looking and listening. He finally spoke up.

'I think we had best leave the kids alone, they'll go live with their uncle until the railroad is finished here. As far as paying or punishment is concerned, your crew had a hand in this whole mess, too. And anyway, when it gets around that these kids can pick up your tracks, you'll all be out of a job."

Everyone laughed again. Paul admired the way these men could make people laugh.

Paul and Jim hit it off right from the start. He and Joseph, it turned out, were both married but had no children. Joseph lived in a little house next to his father's cabin. Jim lived a little farther out on the point, also in a very nice home.

"So, how long are you here for?" Jim asked. Paul didn't have an answer, so he just shrugged. "Anything to get back to in California?"

"Not really." Paul scratched his chin. "Why, need something fixed?"

CHAPTER FOUR

It had been a long day. Paul didn't know if they went to bed late or not, but he didn't care. After having chatted for a while with Jim, Paul and Dad had gone over to Joseph's for the night. The furniture had been rearranged so they could lay out their sleeping bags. Paul noticed Mary had tagged along. Evidently, she gave up her bed to Uncle Joe and would be sleeping at Joseph's as well.

Since it was impossible to remove his clothes without her being able to see, Paul decided to sleep in his shorts and t-shirt. He rolled out his pad, removing his sleeping bag from his duffel. It was a triple-layered bag, which allowed him to use the top layer for warm weather, the center for when it got cooler out, and the lower layer for when it was unbearably cold. Because they were sleeping in the house, Paul would only need to use the first of the three. Once he had it laid out straight, he sat on it to take off his shoes, stockings and shirt. He put the stockings and folded shirt under the upper portion of the bag to use as a pillow, then he scooted himself down in the bag, removed his pants, folded them and put them with his shirt as a pillow. All they had to do now was turn out the lights.

The Innocent Beaver of Big Black River

Soon everything was quiet. Paul fell into a restful sleep, remaining in the same position all night. The next morning he awoke and looked over at his Dad, whose eyes were open.

"How long have you been awake?"

"Oh, I just woke up."

"Where is everybody?"

They got out of their sleeping bags, dressed in a hurry, and ran out the door to the dining hall. There were people leaving, having finished their meals. Uncle Joe and Ray were still sitting there, sipping coffee. Dad looked at Ray and Joe, confused.

"Why didn't you wake us?"

"We wake no one here, that way everyone does what they want, when they want," Ray said. "It's a kind of code we carry on from the old days."

Paul and Dad were lucky at least to get toast, a couple of eggs and coffee. After breakfast they returned to Ray's cabin. Ray told them how he and a brother from the church traveled the northern rivers and lakes and ended up at Big Black River. The northern trek was uneventful, he claimed, going from one native village to another, preaching the word. There was no map. They just went wherever the last village sent them. This was how they found their way to Big Black River.

Just like everywhere they had been before, in Big Black River there were only natives there. Mofet watched him for a long time. One day she followed him. When he noticed her following, she stopped and stood there. If he wanted her he would have to walk back to where she was. It was a sign of their commitment to each other.

She was a princess and was wanted by many others. He didn't want to have trouble with the others, but she chose him and steered him to her father. After a few minutes of awkward silence, Ray spoke up and finally got her father's permission to marry her. The Christian brother Ray had traveled with performed the ceremony.

They lived together for quite a while. Ray, missing the city, decided to take her to Winnipeg to show her around, to try to convince her to make the move to his hometown. They walked around for a while taking in the tall buildings and glittering sidewalks. When she had to go to the bathroom and pay a quarter to open the stall door she made up her mind about Winnipeg.

"Let's go home," she said. "There, I don't have to pay to go to the toilet."

Ray liked to talk about Big Black River. He explained that most of the communication there was done by action; he learned that when someone spoke, it meant more. Some food came in on the ship, and they planted a small garden for vegetables, though the animals ate most of it. Their meat was whatever they could shoot. The waterbed there was muskeg, which was the reason the water looked like tea, and how the river got its name. There was a lot of water up country, good for moose and once in a while a bear; caribou didn't usually come down this far.

They didn't get out much in winter. Everything froze: the river, the lake, except for the center. It could get dangerous, that kind of cold, Ray told them. You had to know your way around.

Over the next few days, Paul and Jim worked together, fixing and preparing for the winter. Paul's experience came in handy, and Jim was able to teach him the way thing worked there. They were proud when they finished; the men slapped each other on the back.

"We're having a dance tonight," Jim said. " You don't have to bring a girl. We only dance for fun. Anyway, there's my wife, Jean, and Mary. They love to dance, and you being new here, I'm sure they'll be all over you. There aren't many new faces. So have fun."

They went there separate ways to eat and get ready. Paul washed, shaved and brushed his teeth in the little kitchen sink. Cleaning up his mess, he put on a clean pair of jeans and a plaid shirt, wiped the mud from his Chippewa boots and walked out the door.

As he left Joseph's house they were all waiting for him. They walked over to a building they called the meeting hall. It was all lit up. Some of the townspeople had musical instruments and had gathered together a makeshift band. They glided around, dancing and laughing. Jean was a real good dancer. Jim didn't seem to mind sharing her out on the floor; he was over with his dad, talking. Paul was used to holding his partner close, but he noticed everyone danced at arms length, so he did the same. He got a few nods of acceptance for his trouble. When the music stopped, Mary approached him.

"Aren't you going to ask me to dance?"

Paul looked at her, the way she glowed in her crisp dress. "I've just been waiting for you to be free."

He grabbed her and whisked her away, spinning across the floor. She held her breath, smiling, then letting herself giggle.

"You can hold me close if you want, no one will mind."

That song finished, but they stayed together for the rest of the evening. As they danced across the floor, Paul noticed a young man about Mary's age sitting in the corner, staring at them. He made no bones about it, watching them everywhere they danced. It made Paul nervous, so he mentioned it to Mary.

"Who is that? He looks like he doesn't like me monopolizing you."

"He lives across the river. He thinks he's my boyfriend, but he's not. He's too plain for me. All he does is sit around, and he wants me to do the same. I may be half Indian, but I'm not going to sit in front of a wigwam the rest of my life." Mary looked up at Paul. "Let's not talk about him. We're having too much fun. Do you like the way I dance?"

"You're like a feather in my arms."

Over on the side, Ray was watching them. He knew his daughter had something on her mind.

Dad had brought a bottle of gin with him to the dance and hid it outside, sneaking out with the other men once in a while for a sip. Everything was fine until someone figured out what was going on; then the bottle emptied fast.

As the party wound down, the musicians put their instruments away and headed for home. Walking home, Mary held on to Paul's arm. Close by, Jim and Jean were doing the same. They all stopped and looked up in the sky, watching the borealis lights flash and wave. It was kind of romantic, Paul thought, holding onto one another to keep warm. Mary looked up at him, then turned away. He thought she has been teasing him all evening. Maybe she was just trying to have a good time. Anyway, she was his cousin, nothing could come of it. And there was Alice, after all.

"Did you have a good time tonight, Mary?"

"I had a wonderful time. I feel bad that they won't do it again until next year."

Jim looked at Paul and winked. Jean thanked Paul for the dance, then they all said goodnight and went their separate ways.

While preparing for bed, Joseph came in to talk to Paul.

"I just don't want to see my sister get hurt, I—" Paul answered before he could continue.

"She's my cousin, and my intentions are to respect her, and everyone here for that matter. If you think I was out of place tonight, just say so."

At that moment Paul's dad came in. He could tell their conversation ended abruptly and knit his brow. Paul shrugged at him.

Over breakfast the next morning, Paul asked Jim how they got around in the winter with the ice and snow.

"The river and lake freeze over, and we use small snowmobiles to get around or haul things. For long trips we go with our neighbor across the river. He's got a Bombardier. Much bigger, takes more people. It gets better mileage, too, and goes faster—thirty, forty miles per hour, depending on conditions. You should see it; the body's flat on the sides, rounded on the ends, big cleats on the treads, holds six of us." Jim was meticulous in describing the Bombardier, just like Paul was about his cars.

Today was Sunday, so everyone was going to church. They all met at the dock, because the church was across the river. The boat was loaded so they had to make only one crossing. The church was small, only holding about fifty people. Paul noticed that the Indians and those of mixed heritage sat in the back rows together, dressed casually but nice. It might have been his imagination, but he felt like they were studying him, like he could feel their stares. Didn't they know he was coming to visit the Pauquettes? It seemed like everyone knew everyone else's business around here. Paul's group sat up in front. Paul slid into a pew, followed by Mary, then Jean and Jim. Uncle Joe sat behind with Dad, Ray, Mofet, Joseph and his wife. When they took their seats Mary sat close to Paul. Paul thought she should have sat closer to Jean, but maybe she had something on her mind.

It was a slow mass. The priest spoke in the native tongue. Paul thought that maybe everyone understood but his group. He paid more attention to the language than the mass; he could have followed the mass in English in his mind, but he didn't. He caught himself and asked the Lord to forgive him. The language was just so fascinating to listen to. It was unlike any other language he had ever heard. He knew it was foolish, but he wondered how people ever figured out how to speak or even understand language like that.

After mass was over the Indians sitting in back were the first to leave, because the door was back there. As Paul's group left, the Indians stood to one side. Their eyes bored holes in Paul. They were just as fascinated by him as he was by them. He thought they must have known Paul's party came from a long ways away. Maybe they'd heard it was a place called California, way out in the United States. They must have been at least a little different than the Canadians who came here once in a while.

The group split up. Ray and Mofet, and Uncle Joe returned to the other side of the river. Dad said Uncle Joe was returning to Selkirk on Captain Sinclair's ship, which had docked earlier that morning. He wanted to get his things together and spend a few minutes alone with Ray.

"If you want," Jim said to Paul, "We can go over to Mr. Jacques's and see his Bombardier. I know you'd like it."

Paul agreed, and the two walked over to the Jacques' place, where the snowmobile was stored in a large one-stall garage. There was no light in there, but with the doors wide open, there was enough light to see what it looked like. Jim explained that it was built on a Model T Ford chassis set backwards on the treads, so the engine would be in the back. It allowed the front to lift so it would climb on top of the snow instead of plowing through it. Also, the reverse gear had more power than the other gears. In the old days, when you came to a steep hill in a Model T, you had to turn around and back up the hill, because you couldn't make it in your forward gears. The Bombardier had tracks like a bulldozer, only they were made out of hardwood cleats. That raised the whole thing up about four feet off the ground, so it wouldn't push the snow. To get in, you had to climb onto the tracks, open a small door that had the original Model T twist handle.

They closed up the garage and returned to the other side of the river. Uncle Joe and Ray were standing there waiting for them. He had his suitcase standing at his feet, ready to go. Paul picked up his bag, and they all walked down to the ship, where they all shook hands, thanked him for everything, wished he didn't have to go. Captain Sinclair came to the landing and motioned to Paul.

"Who knows, maybe I'll be seeing you soon, but just in case, you and your Dad have a good safe trip on your way home. If you ever come back this way, look me up."

Ray asked what that was all about. Dad turned to him.

"Paul must have made a big impression on him when he steered the ship all the way here," he said, watching the steamer sail off and vanish into the distance.

Paul and his Dad were now alone with their cousins. When and how they would get back, Paul wondered, and what was going to happen now? And why didn't they leave with Uncle Joe?

Paul's Dad took him by the arm and started walking back to the cabin.

"The other night when I came into Joseph's house, and the conversation stopped, what was that all about? I saw by your eyes that you couldn't tell me then."

"When Mary started dancing with me, she stayed with me the rest of the evening. I thought she just liked the way I danced, up close like. And maybe she wanted attention. Joseph I guess thought we were being too intimate.

"It was her idea. I kind of went along with her, so as not to hurt her feelings. I mean, I enjoyed it, I had a good time. And you must have seen how she hung onto my arm all the way back to their house, and how today she sat real close to me in church. Maybe she likes me because I'm her cousin and wants to have a good time while I'm here. They don't get many relations to come up here. She probably just feels safe with me is all. In any case, I know we're just visiting."

"No matter what happens, just don't hurt her. She's also a lot younger than you and probably thinks you'd be a good catch. And you would be too, if it weren't for Alice."

Somehow, Paul had forgotten about Alice.

"If you have no intentions towards her, let her down easy. These relatives are being very good to us, considering what they have here."

Paul seized on the opportunity to change the subject.

"Actually, I want to talk to you about that. I'm concerned about paying our way here, not taking advantage. How much do you think we should give them?"

"I know you want to do the noble thing, but you've got to look at it this way: it's like a celebration, us coming here to visit. It's special, and to tell them we want to pay them would be an insult. Maybe when we get home we can do something for them. Maybe they can come visit us. Either way, let's worry about that later.

"As for Mary, you know she's taken, too. She's got a guy who's sweet on her, and I hear his dad is well to do in these parts."

"You mean Mr. Jacques."

"You know him?"

"He was at the dance, sitting in the corner. Mary said he thinks she's his girlfriend, but she thinks he's too slow for her."

"Mr. Jacques bought the land across the river. He built his buildings and made his mark here. Does more than commercial fishing here. He helps to control the community, helps those in need, not to mention how good a friend he is of Ray's. Like I said before, be careful."

"Not to change the subject, but—"

This made Dad laugh. "Right."

"But don't you think we should write to Mom and let her know how things are going here, maybe give her an idea of when we'll be home?"

"I'll do it tonight. The plane picks up the mail tomorrow."

"A plane comes here?" Paul hadn't recalled seeing any.

"Unless there's something to pick up, which usually there isn't, the plane just drops the mail from the air."

By now they had reached the cabin and sat on the bench. It was sure a nice day, Paul thought. Jim saw them and came over.

"Tomorrow we're going moose hunting. Would you two like to come along?"

Paul and Dad looked at one another.

"Sure," Paul said. "But we didn't bring any guns."

"We have everything we need."
"How about hunting licenses?"
"We'll tell them your just sight seeing."
They all laughed.
"Don't worry, we've got you covered."

CHAPTER FIVE

By dawn, frenzy had already descended upon the cabin as everyone gathered their gear and carried it to the dock. Jim and Joseph's canoes were tied there and were being loaded with camping gear and rifles. Both Paul and Dad had been on expeditions before for native trout, but this was going to be different and exciting. Paul helped as much as he could without getting in the way. Following their instructions, Paul would be in one canoe with Jim, and Dad would be in the other with Ray and Joseph.

Looking up, Paul saw Mary coming down the path with her camping gear. Ray looked at her as she stood there.

"Men only on this one."

Without a word, she spun around and went back the way she came.

Paul didn't quite understand why things were done that way here. As if expecting an answer, he looked at Jim, who just looked back at him without saying a word, instead motioning for Paul to get into the canoe and untie the rope. Getting in back of it, he pushed off. They were on their way.

They paddled upstream, gliding along without much effort. About half an hour into the trip, they came to a large pond with a waterfall. They pulled up to a landing and stopped. Unloading the canoes and carried their gear and canoes up the hill to the upper landing, then packed up and set off once more.

The current was a little stronger here, so Paul dug in with his paddle, splashing Jim a few times in the process. Turning in his seat, he looked at Jim, who gave him that certain smile that said he'd better not to do it again. Jim's boat was now quite a distance ahead of the other. As he rowed, he spoke in low tones.

"You hold the paddle this way and steer the canoe as you row. If you stop paddling to make a correction, you'll lose your forward momentum. And no splashing."

Paul laughed. Jim didn't.

"Don't creak your seat or hit your feet up against the inside of the canoe. Don't drop anything into the water. Gun or paddle. Plan ahead. No sudden shifts or movements." He was stern, but didn't mean to offend, knowing Paul wasn't experienced in their way of doing things. "There will be times when I will talk very soft, so listen up. Other times I'll signal with my hands or the paddle, like I might tap it or slide it against the canoe. So you'll have to feel for it. Sliding means quiet."

Jim noticed Paul was looking at the beautiful scenery and was drinking in every moment of it. He was taking in landmarks so if he passed this way again, he wouldn't get lost. They turned this way and that, following the river. Around every bend there was something new to see and admire. He scanned the line of trees for animals and birds. The ducks and loons were easy to see in the water, all around them. The loons made a gurgle that echoed across the water. When they got close, the loons would dive under the water and come up a safe distance away, or they would take off, wings flapping and feet running across the surface of the river. His mind was like a camera, photographing everything. Jim cleared his throat.

"I know you've been hunting before, but a few pointers to sharpen your wits, things to look for."

Paul sighed, but he listened as Jim let forth another litany of advice.

"You mostly look for movement, then you can see animals who are camouflaged, possibly standing right there in front of you. Look for an outline, something that doesn't fit. It's like putting a puzzle together. Or look for their eyes, they'll be looking at you. Then there's smell. Humans give off a scent, which animals can detect."

Paul didn't see how this part differed from the hunting he was used to, but he didn't mention it to Jim.

In the middle of the river, the canoe abruptly stopped. Water was going by on both sides, but they weren't moving. Paul turned to Jim, who had his paddle across his lap. It was as though they were suspended in air.

"Get out," Jim said. Paul must not have responded fast enough, because again he said,

"Get out. Get out of the canoe, Paul."

Paul thought he had to be kidding. If I get out, he said to himself, I'll be taken away with the current. That just doesn't make sense. On the other hand, Jim seemed to know what he was doing, maybe he's testing me to see if I trust him.

Paul put his foot out of the canoe and into the water. To his surprise, the water was only a few inches deep. They were hung up on a large flat rock. He pushed on the rock with his foot and moved the canoe off the rock. They were on there way again. Jim laughed.

"I wouldn't make you swim, I like you better than to do that to you."

Paul breathed a sigh of relief, knowing Jim had been playing a little joke, that he was just having fun with him. His nerves still twitching a little, Paul tried to take his mind off the idea of almost drowning, and the embarrassment he would feel if Jim realized he'd been so thoroughly fooled.

"So where'd you learn to shoot?" Jim asked.

"Army. And I've been shooting ever since."

Jim had him pull a rifle from their packs. It was a 30/30 Winchester, lever action. It looked pretty well worn out but clean, and the action was smooth as Paul checked to see if it was loaded. It didn't have a telescopic scope, so the shooter would have to use open sights. Paul had the same rifle at home. He preferred a larger caliber with a scope; where he hunted, most of his shots were a long way off. He assumed the rifle was sighted in, though, and hoped it shot straight. He wasn't particularly impressed, but he held it in his hands like he was, to please Jim. Likely it was just a spare that they loaned to visitors.

Jim pulled the canoe to the shore and steadied it. "Without getting out of the canoe, let me see if you can hit that small branch hanging out over the water, the one with the leaf on the end of it."

"You mean the one straight ahead of us?"

"Right."

The shot was about 100 yards away and he was sitting in a jiggling canoe

"You've got to be kidding."

"Try it."

Paul checked the rifle to be sure it was loaded, lifted it to his shoulder, steadied it, sighted on the branch and squeezed the trigger. To his surprise, the leaf fell into the water. Now he was impressed. Maybe the rifle wasn't so bad, after all. He was going to have fun with it. He turned and looked at Jim, who nodded and smiled. It could have been a lucky shot, but it proved there was possibility there.

Jim started out again, moving right along with Paul's help. In the process, Paul checked the rifle again. All of a sudden a mallard duck took off, skimming the water. Paul lifted the rifle, sighted the duck and fired. The duck splashed into the water. Jim immediately turned the canoe, paddling towards the duck and picking it up out of the water. The head was gone. Impossible.

To make a shot like that with a rifle was one in a million. Now, he thought, he was as good as Annie Oakley or Wild Bill Hickok. He had to have this rifle. He would offer to buy it from Jim no matter what it cost. Well, within reason. Then he thought, no, he wouldn't ask to buy it. Maybe it was rude here to do such a thing.

The group continued on at a good pace until they came to a fork in the river. Paul's boat took the left fork while Dad's went to the right. Soon they couldn't see each other.

"I know what your plan is," Paul said. "By splitting up we have a better chance of getting a moose."

The river came together again, only it was wider. They stopped on the left shore and watched as the others stopped on the opposite bank. In no time at all, the tents were up and the fires were blazing, sleeping bags and gear safely tucked away in the tents. They had a good spot, level on grass with a view up and down the river.

Paul whittled a stick about the size of a broom handle. He cleaned the duck. It looked good. Putting the stick through it, he smeared the duck with butter, salt and pepper, then suspended it over the fire. He turned it periodically so it would cook on all sides without burning. It cooked up real good. It looked like a Cornish hen. This was going to be a treat. He offered Jim some, but he refused, saying he had something else already prepared for himself. The duck was pretty small, but Paul ate what he could.

After finishing, they cleaned the area and prepared their beds. It was early, so they sat on a log next to the fire and talked.

"Tell me about the city where you live, Paul. What's it like?"

Paul told him about the freeways moving so many cars, but being jammed up all the time because of accidents and gawkers looking for injured bodies laying around. He told him about the houses built on top of one another. In California, the name of the game was money. Those that had it, kept it. There were a lot of murders, rapes and burglaries. People were very unhappy and disgusted with the system. They would vote for something good only to have it knocked down by some corrupt judge. You had to keep your doors locked. If you hurt or killed someone who was robbing you, you could go to jail instead of him. And the cost of living was high. In most families it took both the husband and wife working to pay the bills. You had to insure everything. Then there was the city, county, state, and federal governments taxing everything you own. The homes were nice, he thought, but most people couldn't afford to own them.

"I often thought of going to the U.S.," Jim interrupted, "But from what you tell me, I think I'll stay right here. The land doesn't belong to us, but we come and go as we please. They must have wild animals there, don't they? The main threat here is the wolves, but they stay away. They pick up our scent and make themselves scarce. Then there are the bears. They sometimes happen upon us or we upon them. They will attack to defend themselves or their young, but most of the time they run off.

"Between the bears and the wolves, which are the most fierce?"

"By far the wolves. They hunt in packs, and come at you from all sides. When they are hungry they attack to get your meat. We keep them thinned out pretty good."

"Most of our animals are in the zoo." Paul paused. "But there are still some up in the hills. They're protected, so we have to buy hunting licenses and tags."

Before they turned in, the subject got around to Mary.

"Mary usually comes along with us, but Pa didn't think it was wise to bring her along this time. He knows she likes you."

"I like Mary, but just as a cousin. I thought she felt the same way. I know I'm different, being from then city. Maybe she is just fascinated by what I represent.

"Well, whatever will be, will be." He patted Paul on the back before scrunching down into his sleeping bag.

They had just gotten comfortable when they heard a large commotion on the other side of the river. They both jumped out of their sleeping bags and ran to the river shore. Looking across, they saw the campfire still burning. About a thousand yards from their parents' campfire there were three bears fighting.

"Jim, maybe we should shoot at them. Bear meat would be good to take back."

"We'll just wait and watch. We came for moose. If we start shooting the moose will go further back in the brush and we will miss out on getting one." He looked at Paul. "You're worried about your Dad. Well, don't be scared. He's in very good hands with Pa and Joseph. Pa taught us everything we know, and he's good out there. Even the Mounties come to him for help."

They stood there for a while before they saw that the bears run off, each taking a different direction into the dark woods.

CHAPTER SIX

When he awoke, Paul saw they were in heavy bog country. The riverbed stretched out before them like a vast sponge. Jim didn't say anything, but kept sniffing the air. Then he would snort, shaking his head before repeating the process. Likely, the others had already woken up and taken off, so they headed upstream again. Canoe loaded, they pushed off, looking for the camp on the other side of the bank. It wasn't there.

The river turned into channels leading in all directions. Paul thought it might be easy to get lost in a place like this, so he paid close attention to the terrain, taking mental notes: a tree here, a rock there. Being with Jim, he would never have to use these things, but he did it anyway. Had he been alone, he would have tied a piece of cloth to a branch or broken a branch periodically along the way, anything to use as a marker.

They were in the canoe all day. Paul would have liked to get out and stretch his legs. He didn't complain, though. If that was what Jim wanted to do, it was good enough for him. He knew Jim must have had a good reason for whatever he was doing. There was food in the canoe, so they ate as they went along.

Night fell and it was cold on the water. They continued on, but now they slowed and were hugging the shore, which had a high bank. It got darker still, and the canoe slowed to just a crawl. So this is how they hunted, Paul thought.

Not a word was spoken. Paul knew Jim was back there, but he might as well have been all alone. He now carried the rifle across his legs. He didn't do much paddling, so as not to interfere with Jim's pace or direction. Darkness continued to descend; Paul could no longer see where they were going. He could see the nose of the canoe, but not the water. There were trees and brush on both sides of the channel but they could be seen only as a silver silhouette cast by the moon; all else was blackness.

Despite it being nightfall, Jim could still guide the canoe with great fluidity. Once in a while a branch would touch Paul's shoulder, startling him. How Jim could maneuver the canoe in this darkness? It was like the canoe was part of him, or he part of it. It did exactly what he wanted it to do.

Paul sat on a seat that measured six inches by a foot. He knew he had a rifle because he could feel it in his hands, but he couldn't see it, nor could he see his own arms. Finally the surface of the water came into focus; he kept his eyes on it, without blinking. Staring for fear it to would go away. There wasn't a sound. If a moose crossed in front of them he wouldn't be able to shoot it. How could he see it? What were they doing here, like this, anyway? This could be dangerous. What would he do if they capsized? Grab the bushes and hang on? And they would lose everything in the water.

All of a sudden he heard the scrape of the paddle. Remembering Jim's instructions, he made himself as silent as possible. He blinked again. If he were alone he would have just turned on a flashlight. He thought he saw something move upstream. Maybe he was mistaken. His eyes were playing tricks on him. No, there it was again. Something moving in the water. But what was it? From what he could tell, it didn't look like anything he had ever seen. He blinked again, trying to improve his focus. It had something sticking up all over. Eight to ten feet long, maybe. About five feet

The Innocent Beaver of Big Black River

tall. It was moving towards them. What was wrong with Jim? Didn't he see it? Why wasn't he doing anything?

Paul felt the paddle rubbing the canoe once more. Could Jim be scared, and not know how to handle this? Paul was in the front of the canoe. He would be the first to make contact with the thing. It would attack him first. It was so dark, how could he fight this thing off?

Then he realized they were still moving forward. Jim's got to be out of his mind, Paul thought. A threat lay ahead, and he's still moving towards it. Maybe he wants to get rid of me. But I didn't do anything to harm anyone, did I? Maybe it was Mary. He should have stayed away from her. It kept coming closer and closer. Paul was about to turn and look at Jim, even though he probably wouldn't be able to see him anyway, when there it was again, that paddle rubbing up against the canoe. Paul felt like screaming. The hell with the paddle. It was almost on top of them. There it was again, that rubbing.

Paul was frozen stiff. His breath was quick. He would have closed his eyes, but he was too scared. He didn't move for fear of falling out of the canoe. It looked like a giant porcupine. It was huge. As it passed, Paul closed his eyes, sure it was waiting to strike. He was done for. He was going to die right here. This monster would eat every part of him and there would be no evidence of what happened to him.

There was a loud slap on the water which jarred Paul's eyes open just in time to see a large beaver dive under the surface of the water. It must have sensed them sitting there in the canoe. The water from the slap the beaver made splashed all over Paul, bringing him to attention.

Beside the boat was a tree. A tree being pulled by a beaver. it was about 6 feet wide and 20 feet long, with its branches sticking up all over the place. Paul was shaking all over. he had to get control of himself. If Jim saw him like this, he would suggest going back to the house, and that would be the end of their vacation. His Dad would be disappointed. Everyone would laugh at him. The big white hunter, scared by a beaver.

Paul took a deep breath and felt Jims paddle on his shoulder. It was just enough pressure to steady him, clear his thoughts. A beaver pulling a tree down a river, right next to him. He could have reached out and touched it. He wouldn't have, of course. But so close. Sure, he knew it was possible to trap a beaver, but to see one within arm's reach was a real rarity. This was probably an everyday thing for someone like Jim, but Paul knew a lot of people who'd give their eye teeth for an experience like this. Jim could have made a tap or something on the canoe, before the beaver got that near to the boat, but perhaps he'd done it for Paul's sake. He would have to remember to thank him.

In the pitch of night, the two continued up the river. Paul could feel Jim maneuvering the canoe ever so slightly. Soundlessly, Jim landed the canoe under a bank that looked as though it shot straight up six feet out of the water, with grass and twiggy trees atop it. Paul felt the faint bump of the oar on the canoe, then the rubbing, all too familiar now. Be alert and very quiet. There was something coming. They stayed there for what seemed like fifteen minutes, or maybe as many hours, but it might've only been fifteen seconds. Paul couldn't be sure.

Jim shot.

It erupted like a canon, and Paul almost lost his rifle. Seconds later there was a big splash, right in front of Paul. A moose had fallen from the bank, as if out of the sky, and landed not more than twenty feet in front of Paul. He was soaked and scared witless. Jim held the canoe so it wouldn't be capsized by the wave, letting out a blood-curdling yell right in Paul's ears.

"We've got to get the moose out of the water and start dressing it out. C'mon, Paul."

Paul was unsure whether he was shivering because he was sopping wet, or because a moose had nearly landed on his head; either way, he wasn't going to move. Jim knew what he was doing. He'd known all along. It was just as well, because Paul wasn't much help in the dark, not to mention the state he was in. He didn't even see the clearing until Jim pulled the canoe into it.

Finally, Paul thought of a way to put himself to use. He tied up the canoe, then helped Jim pull the moose onto the shore. Jim started with his knife and the moose seemed to fall apart. The entrails were pulled off a distance away from the carcass. Jim handed Paul a large piece of gut with the heart and liver.

"Wrap it and put it in the canoe."

Paul turned and almost fell over Joseph, who was now working along with Jim. He didn't see or hear him and the others pull up in the dark. Daybreak was starting, which made it a little easier. In what seemed like no time at all, they had the moose skinned out quartered, the meat wrapped in its skin and packed in the canoes.

Now that they had their moose, Paul thought, they could relax and take their time going back. Dad's canoe headed out first. Jim told Paul to keep his rifle close. Paul thought this might have been in case they encountered another moose. But then how would they carry another one out of here? They were packed to capacity, and it seemed like they couldn't take anymore. Once in the water and on their way, Jim let out a sigh of what Paul thought was relief. The hunt was over.

They moved along at a good pace, using the current, not taking too many chances on flashy maneuvers. The further down stream they got, the faster the current was; they took advantage of it, turning this way and that. Paul was having a good time again. They approached the waterfalls. Boy, that was fast, Paul thought. Already they weren't far from home. Jim somehow passed the others and was reaching the landing above the falls first. As he reached the landing, Paul jumped out of the canoe with the rope to tie it up, but the current took the boat faster than he could hitch it to something. The nose of the canoe caught in a rock cropping; it looked as if it was about to tear the vessel in half. Everything would have gone over the falls, including Jim, who was still somehow calm and collected.

"Push the canoe off and hold on to the rope."

Paul had to react fast; it was up to him this time around. He did as Jim instructed, and the canoe made an outward swing, landing them down the shore. Jim hopped out of the canoe, as if he'd choreographed it. Once again, Paul found himself trembling.

The others pulled up behind them, tied up and started unloading.

"Take your rifle with you and wait for us at the bottom," Ray said.

Paul and Dad headed out. Paul set his load down and started to head back.

"You better take your rifle with you," Dad repeated.

Paul grabbed it and headed up the hill, passing Ray, Jim and Joseph on the way. He reached the top and was picking up another load when he something caught his eye, moving very fast, coming right at him. He dropped his load and picked up his rifle. They were the size of bears, only running like dogs. Then it struck him. Timberwolves.

They must have found the moose carcass and followed them from there. The scent of the meat packed in the canoes coming down the river must have been easy to follow. Now Paul knew why they wanted them to keep their rifles close, but wished they had been a little more specific as to why.

The wolf pack was coming at full speed through the woods, dodging trees, leaping over logs, darting back and forth. My God, Paul thought, the size of them. He shot the first one, then just kept pumping the lever action and shooting as fast as he could. He was anxious and missed a few, but he thought he saw most of them go down. There wasn't time to take aim. They came from all directions. Some he knew he killed. Some he wounded. Inside he felt like screaming but he knew he had to make every shot count or he was a goner. He kept pumping and shooting. Then he noticed no bullets were coming out. He was out of bullets.

Still he kept pumping, hoping there was one more round in there somewhere. A wolf charged at him, hitting a mound of dirt to give it lift, to strike him head on in the chest, knocking him down where the others could help tear him apart.

It all happened so fast. He was standing there trying to shoot, not hearing anything, when shots rang out from behind him. It was as if he'd been transported into a shooting gallery. He took a chance, turning his head to look. Joseph's shot caught the wolf in the chest, Jim's shot hit it in the head. The wolf seamed to disintegrate in mid air. Paul twisted to one side, letting the wolf fall at his feet. There in a line were Jim and Joseph firing away. It was all over. Timberwolves were lying all over the place.

Paul had reached his limit. He was about to go mad. He didn't want them to see him like this, so he clenched his teeth, picked up his load and headed down the hill. When he got to the bottom his Dad was there to greet him.

"What happened up there? Sounded like everyone was emptying their rifles." He grinned.

Paul knew if he started talking, he would lose it. So instead he shrugged, put down his load, turned around and headed back up the hill. He wasn't used to this. He wanted to hide under a rock if he could. At least there was still a lot more of the meat and gear to bring down. He thought if he kept busy, the fear might go away. As he passed the others going up the hill, they looked him over.

"You okay?" Jim asked.

"Sure." He kept going.

When he got to the bottom with the last of the cargo, both canoes were loaded. Before they pushed off, they decided to take a break by the shoreline. Paul felt a little calmer now, and he asked what were they going to do with the wolves.

"Scavengers will get 'em," he said.

"That's not how we do things." Ray replied. "We'll string them up in the trees and come back for them later. We can use the fur and teeth."

As they climbed up the hill, Dad and Paul surveyed the wolf carcasses.

"Boy, you must have had the hell scared out of you," Dad said.

"Oh, no," Paul answered. "I didn't have time to be scared. I was too busy."

The river carried them right along. Soon they were approaching the dock at Ray's place. There was a bunch of friends waiting for them; they must have heard the gunshots. The group rushed the dock and began helping them unload.

"I'd like you and your Dad to eat with us tonight," Ray said.

Paul accepted. He was feeling a bit better now; he took up his bundle and followed along with the group to the shed, where meat was being packed in layers of ice and sawdust to preserve it for the harsh winter that would undoubtedly be coming.

Paul and his Dad ate at Ray's that evening. Mofet was polite but quiet. The food was good, and Paul hadn't eaten for quite a while, so he had plenty of helpings. His appetite was a hit with Mofet and Mary, who watched every move he made. After his talk in the woods with Jim, Paul decided he was going to try to ignore Mary.

After dinner, Ray was watching the window. A group of people was gathered outside. Ray went out to see what they wanted. Paul watched as Ray stood and talked to them a minute before coming back in the house.

"They want to see you," Ray said, pointing at Paul.

Paul's eyes bulged. Could he have done something wrong? Were they going to lynch him or tar and feather him?

"What do they want?"

"I don't know, but you had better go out there. They won't go away until you do."

There were about twenty of them, and Jim was there. They surrounded him, and to Paul's surprise, they had smiles on their

The Innocent Beaver of Big Black River

faces. Before he could blink they were patting him on the back, welcoming him, gasping in awe over the wolves he'd killed. Paul held his hand up.

"I only did what any one of you would've done. The real heroes here are Jim and Joseph and their dad. They saved my life."

After the group cleared, Jim turned to him.

"You don't understand. These people know that you don't come from these parts, yet you stood up to the wolves and did your share in protecting us. If they had made it over the hill by the falls, they would have caught the village by surprise. We would have got some of them but there would have been a whole lot more bloodshed, and not all of it wolf's blood."

"I still want to thank you and Joseph for saving my life back there."

"Well, thank you, too."

Mary and Dad both looked at Paul with stars in her eyes as he returned to the cabin.

"Jim told me you saved him from going over the falls," Dad said. "You seem to have taken to this lifestyle pretty quickly. I'm proud of you, but like I said before, please be careful. Your mother wouldn't let me in the house if I came home without you."

At that they all laughed.

"I only did what they told me to do. Jim just used me to save himself." He chuckled to himself. "I like Jim. Did he tell you about the beaver? Evidently, he was stalking the moose in the pitch dark, don't ask me how. The moose had been walking along the shore, possibly looking for a place to cross the channel. Jim made sure I didn't make a sound. He just glided his canoe expertly along, following the moose without alerting it. We were so quiet that an unsuspecting beaver swam down the river towards us pulling a tree with out sensing we were there until it was right next to us. Then it hit the water and dove under. But he let me see it, he knew I'd want to see it and he didn't scare it off."

Paul smiled to himself. "I don't know what my future is going to be, but I hope Jim's in it."

Father and son sat quietly for a while, drifting slowly towards sleep.

The next morning everyone sat around the table talking about the hunt and thinking about another one.

"We're thinking of leaving," Dad said.

They all stopped talking and looked at one another as if the world had come to an end. Finally, Ray broke the awkward silence.

"I'll get you back to Selkirk. Peter will take you to Winnipeg where you can take a plane to Los Angeles, but we would like Paul to stay with us a while longer."

He knew it was an offer Paul wouldn't refuse. Paul looked at his Dad.

"You want to stay on, don't you?"

Saying no would have meant they didn't appreciate their kindness and consideration, so Paul nodded. Paul would stay and Dad would go. Dad would check on Paul's truck as he went by Peters place. There was a passenger steamer that was going by the next day, heading south from the Norway House to Selkirk. They would take Dad out to the steamer in one of the fishing boats. The steamer would stop and pick up Dad. Paul once they were alone asked his Dad.

"Is it all right, you going home alone?

"After what we've been through in the last few days, being alone on a boat shouldn't be a problem at all. At least this one I don't have to paddle."

As they settled into a routine, Jim and Paul followed one another around like puppies. At his suggestion, Jim had set up a room for Paul at his place. Paul was unsure of whether or not this had anything to do with Mary, but he made no mention of it. Paul was good at splitting and stacking wood, and Jim was good at knowing when to put another log on one of the fires.

Working together, it didn't take long to get everything done and keep everyone warm. The boats were pulled up on shore and winterized. Any patchwork that needed to be done on the houses was taken care of. After a few days of steady work they got caught up and had nothing to do, so they found themselves sitting around trying to make work.

Paul felt a little out of place sometimes. He noticed Joseph stayed close to his father. He could see them talking, but what about he couldn't make out. When he was close to them they didn't say much, or they changed the subject. Jean and Mary were always together, so Mary spent much of her time at Jim's.

As time went on, Paul and Mary went for the occasional walk together; once in a while they held hands. One evening Jim called them outside. There was a beautiful borealis in the sky. They stood there watching it for a while before it was time for Paul to walk Mary back to the other cabin. It was getting darker.

As they approached the door, Mary turned to Paul, and they kissed. She looked into Paul's eyes, searching for some response. Apparently not finding what she expected, Mary quickly said goodnight and closed the door behind her.

When Paul turned to go back to Jim's, Jim was standing there, waiting for him.

"You and Mary are getting pretty serious. Remember our talk?"

"I don't know what to do. Being close to her all day every day doesn't help. I don't want to ignore her. I want to be friendly and kind to her, but I think she wants more than that. Doesn't she see her friend across the river? I'm confused, kind of caught between a rock and a hard place."

"They were seeing one another before you came. Everyone thought they were going to get married, but you changed all that." Jim's face was getting red. "Now she's after you, and she's more than a little disappointed with your lack of response. Everyone's waiting . I saw her kiss you."

Paul stared back at Jim. He had nothing to say for himself. He thought everyone wanted him to stay away from her, and he'd tried. Wasn't that the right thing to do, to say no? What about things back home?

"Say, are you ready to go hunting again?" Jim asked.

"Huh?" Paul was unprepared for the sudden change of subject.

"The natives say they hear the moose calling, and if they don't go now, they won't have meat for next year. They also say that you bring good luck, and they want you to go along with them. They won't take no for an answer. They'll come here and ask you themselves if necessary. You're big medicine to them."

Paul thought it was a good idea; getting away would slow things off a little between him and Mary. It would give them time to think. Maybe she would go back across the river and things would be changed when he returned from the trip. Paul had waited a long time to marry, a little longer wouldn't hurt.

CHAPTER SEVEN

The next morning early they left as a large group, following one another. Given their large number, the portage at the falls was easy this time around. The Indians were quick. Had plenty of stamina. Everything was automatic. It wasn't a race, but to see them move, one might have thought otherwise. One of them made like he was going to pick up Paul and put him in his canoe; they all laughed.

They traveled faster than Jim's group had. They weren't interested in sightseeing or bird watching. They played follow-the-leader and stayed at the same camp that Paul and Jim used. Nights were a lot shorter, so they didn't have the cover of darkness to surprise a moose. With the large group, they would have to use another method on this hunt. Their intentions were to get as many moose as possible. Paul figured he'd sit back and see how they did it.

The channels went in all directions. Each canoe took a channel. The one on the end would make a moose call similar a female's. The bull moose would hopefully move to answer her. When they crossed the channels they would be picked off. Everyone had to get into position fast, before the call was made.

Valmore Valiquette

There would be only one chance today. If they missed they would have to camp and try again tomorrow, and it would only get harder as the days wore on, as the moose would inevitably catch on. Jim and Paul were in position at their favorite spot, waiting and resting. They had finally relaxed when they heard the call. It was a long distance away, but they could hear it so clearly, the hair stood on the back of Paul's neck. Had he not known it was one of their own, Paul would have been sure it was a real wild moose.

They paddled with all their might to meet the noise head on. As they rounded a bend in the river they saw two bull moose fighting in the river, decimating the surrounding woods with their giant antlers.

"Take the one on the right," Jim said.

They both fired at the same time, sending both creatures to the ground. First they twitched, then all was silent and still. Jim stood up in the canoe and let out his whooping call. Tying a rope around a moose antler, he then affixed the other end to a tree and tied it off. With another rope, they tied the antlers of the other one and started pulling it out of the water. When Paul and Jim examined their moose, they looked at one another. Paul's shot caught his moose in the eye, shattering its brain. Jim's moose was hit behind the ear. The bullet shattered the base of the scull, right at the spinal cord. There was no loss of meat on either one.

Altogether, the men took down four moose on their expedition, three bulls and a cow. The cow was accidently shot as she came charging out of the woods at one of the canoes. With as much meat as they had they didn't need the cow, but it was self-defense. And it certainly wouldn't go to waste.

With twelve men all working together, they made short work of butchering and cleaning up the area. They were all in high spirits, whooping and joking. They slapped Paul on the back for bringing them good luck. The canoes packed, they headed back down the river. If there were any wolves in the area they didn't show. It was easy going, and soon Paul found himself feeling free enough to make small talk.

"Does everyone have a hunting license?" he asked Jim.

"Indians don't need one, and the others would have to go to Norway House to get one. You don't have to worry. It's not like you're not going to take a trophy or meat home to the states."

"But what if someone finds out?"

"If they ever hear of this, the worst they'll say is, 'So, you had a good year.' They probably won't like the idea of our shooting the cow, but they know the Indians frown on it even more than they do. After all, they believe the cow replaces what they take from the land; they respect her so she will provide for them in the future."

When they reached the factory they stopped at Ray's place; they were unloading the cow when he came down to meet them. When he saw what they got he was overjoyed, but when he saw them unloading the cow, his face changed.

"No."

"Cow belongs to him," one of the Indians said, pointing to Paul.

All eyes were on him. He had no choice but to accept.

Before they left, most of the Indians approached Paul, thanking him for bringing them luck on their hunt. Paul shook all their hands, returning their thanks before they pushed off in their canoes.

What a beautiful sight to see, Paul thought. Five canoes, a small armada of friends following one another. Paul felt a lump in his throat. Turning to Jim, he smiled, choking back a tear.

"We sure had a lot of fun, huh? It's like the beaver: it only happens once in a lifetime."

"Let's go see if we can find something to eat." So they headed towards his house.

As they entered, they noticed that the girls were waiting for them. They must have seen them coming. The table was set with a white tablecloth and their special dishes. They were famished and proceeded to sit down.

"Oh, no. You have to wash and change your clothes."

They both stood, looking at one another; they were hungry and tired.

"What's the big deal, Jean?" Jim asked.

"Mary cooked a special diner all by herself, for Paul—" Jean paused with a certain amount of purpose after uttering his name. "And she wants everything just right. "

They had to agree if they expected to eat. After all, their clothes were dirty and full of blood, not to mention the smell they were emitting. Jim and Paul took turns washing and then went to there rooms to change

They returned to the table, where candles had now been lit.

"Sit, please," Mary said.

Mary started out by saying grace, then proposing a toast with grape juice.

"We're both so happy that you both returned safely from your hunting trip. One of the Indians told us how many moose you got, and we're so proud. We are pleased to have Paul here with us," she looked him straight in the eye. "And I hope you stay for ever."

Paul smiled. At first he felt a little embarrassed; did she really think he had made a commitment to her? All he did was kiss her, and it was a casual kiss at that. He had quite a loving feeling for her, but with her family looking on he didn't know how to react. She'd put the ball in his court, and it might be his last chance to do things his way.

"I want to thank you and Jim and Jean, for this wonderful dinner," he started, raising a glass. "I also want to thank your whole family for accepting me here. I wish this could have happened to me a long time ago."

Jim indicated he wanted to start eating but Paul set down his glass, raised his hand and continued.

"Mary, will you marry me?"

Everyone, even Mary, was stopped dead in their tracks.

"Yes."

There were tears in her eyes. They went to one another and kissed and hugged. By this time both Jim and Jean were up and coming around the table. They congratulated them both. Now both girls were wiping the tears away.

"Now," Jim said, "Can we eat?"

They all laughed and sat down. Paul didn't know if it was proper but he had a Saint Christopher's medallion on his key chain. He removed it and gave it to Mary.

"Sorry I don't have a ring. I'll replace it with a real one later."

Jim leaned across the table.

"You've not only made Mary happy today, but our whole family. We're proud to have you with us."

Paul knew he had done the right thing. His life would be different now, but they could go down country once in a while, possibly in the winter. His Mom and Dad could come up for the summer. They could build a nice house next to Jim's.

Dinner was delicious: moose meat roast with potatoes, carrots and onions picked fresh from the garden. Jean explained that the plants would survive there all winter under a canvas covered with straw. The snow would cover the straw, keeping the ground warm enough so the plants wouldn't freeze. For desert Mary had prepared a nice chocolate cake with a white syrup like topping. She could really cook.

While the girls were cleaning up, Paul and Jim sat in a corner talking.

"How come you decided to ask Mary tonight to marry you?"

"Well, I wasn't. I think the girls must have put something in the grape juice." He laughed at his own joke. "No, just kidding. I fell in love with Mary the first time I saw her, but she being my cousin, well—to be honest, I thought it'd create a little more of a problem. It's still something that has to be worked out. I mean, our love can't bring misery to our children."

Everyone in the cabin was now paying attention.

"Explain," Jim said.

"Well, you know. If two relatives have a child together, it could be—it could be deformed. I've heard some churches won't even marry people who are related in any way. And we're second cousins."

It seemed like Mary wasn't listening. She wasn't going to let anything spoil the evening for her. She came out of the bedroom with the St. Christopher medallion hanging around her neck on a string. In her hands she had both their coats.

"Now we have to go and tell Mother and Father."

Jim saw them to the door, indicating that they should go alone. As they stepped out he looked at the sky. There was a chill in the air.

"We got back just in time. Otherwise we would have had a real storm to contend with."

Jim and Jean would have gone to the cabin with them to celebrate, and Jim knew his father liked Paul, but you never knew what his reaction would be, so Jim thought it best they keep it a smaller affair.

Paul and Mary walked holding one another towards the cabin. Joseph came out from the shed.

"Just a minute. This has got to stop,. You both can't go on like this. "

"Please," Mary said. "Come with us into the cabin. We have something to say to Mom and Dad."

They both went along inside. Her mother and father were sitting side-by-side at the table. Dinner was over and everything was cleaned up. They had a candle only for light. They were holding hands.

"Paul asked me to marry him, and I accepted."

The air was still. Joseph tried to speak.

"Wha?"

Ray went over and shook Paul's hand. Mofet hugged Mary. She also had tears in her eyes. They both looked at one another.

"Is this really what you want, Mary?" Mofet asked.

"Oh yes, since I first saw him."

"Congratulations," Ray said. "Welcome to my family."

Joseph was standing aside. When the time was right he came over and shook Paul's hand, congratulating him, then hugged Mary and looked over her shoulder at his father. Paul noticed this but put it in the back of his mind. Mofet came to him and stood for a minute; then, seeming to make up her mind, she reached out and drew him in to her. She was soft and delicate. Now Paul knew why Ray married her.

Joseph remained expressionless. He stood back, smiling as though he had to. However, no one paid him much attention. There were coffee and sweet cakes to be enjoyed, and more accolades for their most recent hunting excursion. Paul hoped they never found out how scared he actually was.

Later, when everyone was leaving, Mary wanted to return to Jim's house with Paul, but her mother held her sleeve and gave her a stare; that took care of that.

At Jim's, Paul lay awake in bed thinking how fast things had changed. He was thirty-one and getting married, or engaged anyway. This trip to help out his Dad had sure turned out different than he expected. He should've been home by now, working at some garage, living in a trailer someplace. He would be seeing Alice. *Alice.* What about her? He thought he loved her. She certainly loved him. But they hadn't been doing so well, had they? No, they hadn't. Maybe that was his fault. They could have made a happy marriage. But that was all gone now.

Mary might have been plainer than Alice, but she had a gorgeous figure. She was healthy, worked hard, and she could run like the wind. A little makeup and he would have to beat the admirers off with a stick. They would need time to plan their wedding date. Maybe a year or two. He would write to his Mom and Dad and tell them the good news.

Paul thought it would be best if they lived in California and maybe came up to Manitoba for vacations. Mary could get a job—no, he would want her to stay home and raise the kids. She'll like that. He laughed at the idea, him and kids. Well, others did it. They should have no problem. And he chuckled a little, thinking how it would be true when he called them 'a bunch of little Indians.' But no one else had better call them that. And if someone else called Mary a stupid Indian he would show them, he would kick them straight into next Tuesday.

Next morning, before Paul was even out of bed, there was someone stomping in through the kitchen door. Looking out from under the covers, he saw her standing there, all bundled up with snow on her feet.

Paul knew the snow was coming but didn't expect it this soon. As usual, he dressed inside his sleeping bag to conceal himself; she sat and watched. As he finished dressing, she removed her boots and coat. He no sooner stood up than she was in his arms. She began whispering in his ear.

"I was up all night thinking of you. We're going to have such a wonderful life together. I've got it all figured out. I'll tell you all about it later when we're alone. You know how I want to get some time alone with you."

"One thing I have to know. Are you the one who used to roll up my sleeping bag and put my things away over at Joseph's?"

She blushed a little.

"I hoped that you would notice." Mary let out another giggle, musical like the one she'd been bursting with that day when they met. "How long are we going to wait before we get married?" She didn't skip a beat. "Let's do it right away. We could cross the river this afternoon. We could go to the cabin in the woods and spend our honeymoon there. We don't have to wait."

Paul had different ideas, but what could he do? He knew how his relationships had been in the past, and he didn't want an all-out war on his hands.

Jim had entered and was standing in the doorway of his bedroom.

"Now listen here, Mary. You can't rush into this like a couple of teenagers. Jean and I waited six months. I wanted to get married right away but she convinced me that we should wait. In the end it turned out for the best, and it gave everyone a chance to get used to the idea."

Mary's shoulders slumped just slightly.

"Mary," he continued. "You'll be married a long time. You want your wedding day to be truly memorable, not just a big blur."

"Jim's right, we should give ourselves a chance to get better acquainted." Paul said.

But Paul had been there better than three months, and he knew what Mary was thinking. He was what she wanted. She felt she knew all she had to know about him. She didn't want to give him a chance to change his mind. She knew he was older than her and heard that older men were harder to tie down. He was glad for Jim's intervention. He would have to remember to thank him later, when Mary was out of earshot.

Mary, heaving a sigh, turned to Jim.

"Ok, you're right, but I won't wait long. I'll start preparing now, and we'll have a nice wedding, you'll see." She held tight to Paul and whispered in his ear. "I'm sorry. I love you."

Crestfallen, Mary put on her boots and coat and went back to the other cabin. Paul was lost for words. The way she left. He looked at Jim.

"She'll get over it. In the old days if an Indian man and woman spent one night in a teepee together, they were bound for life. We're only half, but we still have to do the right thing. I hope you understand."

Paul coughed.

"Oh, no, you're right. I agree completely."

Jean prepared breakfast, which was eaten in silence. As the dishes were being cleared, Paul leaned back in his chair.

"Jim, got to talk to you about something."

"We have to get our winter equipment ready and button things up before the freeze. We can talk then."

Paul didn't have any cold winter clothes or boots. He was going to suggest they try to get to the Norway House where he could buy some, but to his surprise, Jim rummaged through his closet and came up with long johns, bib overalls, shirts and a well-worn jacket. The boots were a little loose, but that was okay, because it meant he could wear an extra pair of stockings. When Paul was dressed Jim handed him a hat and a warm pair of gloves.

With that they went out in the snow; by now it was really coming down. They made their way to the shed, unlatched the door and forced it open, pushing the snow out of the way. There were snow shovels hanging on the wall. They each took one and started shoveling paths around the shed, up to the house, then over to the cabin. Mary waved at them through the window. They stopped and waved back. She was all smiles. You just can't tell about women, Paul thought.

They continued shoveling a path to Ray's shed and over to Josephs house, where Joseph came to the door.

"You don't have to do that."

"Just trying to have some fun," Jim answered.

Making their way back to Jim's, the men left the shovels by the door so they could shovel their way back to the shed if the blizzard got worse.

"Ok, let's talk," Paul started." I've been here for three months now. I know all about hospitality. I don't know what arrangements were made. I don't know who paid for them. However, I do know

The Innocent Beaver of Big Black River

that up here there aren't many things to buy, but what there is costs money. I want to pay my keep. I want a financial agreement, if not to reimburse you for my expenses, then to make me feel I am paying my way. It just doesn't feel right, you being so nice for nothing. Like these cloths , no one has ever loaned me his coat before."

"Without the coat you'd freeze, and then who could I get to help me do my work?" Both men laughed at that. "I'll tell you what. I'll think it over what you've said. I knew you'd bring this up someday, and I hoped to put it off as long as possible. Because really, we feel like we owe you, not the other way around. You don't let us treat you like a guest. You pitch in, and you want to do things our way. It's hard to find a man like that, especially one who's not from here. We don't really think money should be an issue between us. But like I said, I'll think it over, and I'd appreciate it if you wouldn't mention any of this to my father."

Paul felt like he just got told off. His Dad told him about this, but he had to make a fool of himself, his own way.

They both turned at the sound of Jean at the door, calling them to lunch. They closed the door to the shed and headed for the house. While they were eating Jean said she went over to the cabin and talked to Mary.

"She thought over what she'd done and felt like a fool. Paul, you've got to talk to her."

"There's a spot you could take her to, out on the point," Jim said, winking at his wife. "It's our spot, but we'll loan it to you. You can see for miles out on the lake. We go there a lot to watch the boats go by in the summer."

"And to hold hands and tell one another how happy we are," Jean added.

After lunch, Paul put on his coat and went out, asking Jim and Jean to wish him luck. Upon arriving at the cabin he asked Mary if she'd like to go for a walk. She immediately accepted and got her coat. Her mother went to get her coat, too, but Ray shook his head, so she put it back.

Mary and Paul headed out towards the point side-by-side. Then Paul put his arm around her, holding her close, so she wouldn't fall down, he told himself. They shuffled along the path, pushing the snow with their boots. There were only a few snowflakes falling now. As they passed Jim and Jean's, they were looking out the window. They ducked out of sight as Paul and Mary passed.

Out at the point there was a log they used as a bench. Jim thinks of everything, Paul thought. The lake hadn't completely frozen over yet. There was ice along the shore, but it was still fragile. There were a few birds and ducks flying around, for the most part the lake was still and serene. They sat for a long time, Paul's arm around Mary, who stared straight ahead. He was going to start a conversation when she turned and looked straight into his eyes, stone-faced.

"Did you really mean to propose to me?"

Here's my chance to get out of this, Paul thought. Probably my last chance. But now he wasn't sure he wanted the out.

"Yes, of course I meant it. We'll have a great life together. We could spend summers here and winters back in Southern California, where it's nice and warm, and there's no snow."

"No snow?"

"Only on top of the mountains. A lot of people go up there to ski. You can go skiing in the morning, then go to the beach in the afternoon and swim in the ocean. No white Christmases there." Paul closed his eyes. "People go to the mountains and fill their pick-ups with snow to put on their front lawns for the kids to play in."

"What's a lawn?"

"Well, it's a lot of work, for one thing. You put fertilizer on it to make it grow. Then you have to tend to it, and care for it. Every one has one. We'll have one. There are a lot of things to see in the city, and someday I'll show you all of it."

She turned to hug him, and as they embraced they kissed each other with abandon, with the passion they had so long had to restrain under the watchful gaze of family. They could feel each other's hearts beating out of their ribcages, as if trying to break free. His hands were moving from one place to another under her clothes. Her breasts were firm, neither too big nor too small. Perfect. He wanted to feel all of her, her smoothness, her warmth. She was gasping for air. Her hands were under his coat, and she felt around for an opening to get inside his clothes. She caressed his body, pulling gently at his hair, lowering her hands to his belt buckle.

He thought he might scream. It was a good thing it was cold out. He glanced over towards Jim's house, expecting to find him and his wife watching. Paul pushed Mary away.

"When you shoot, you take aim. And I'm not ready to shoot you yet. We have to save this."

"Oh, shoot me. Shoot me," she laughed. She didn't want to let go.

Paul got up, then turned to help Mary. The brushed themselves off and headed back to the house. If he had followed her lead, he thought, they would have to get married tomorrow. Paul wondered if she would level off, or if she would wear him out.

"What are you smiling about, Paul?"

"I was just thinking if our sex life would be always as passionate. You know I have a bad heart, and I don't know if I could last with that much excitement."

She socked him softly on the arm.

"Oh, you."

And then they were in each other's arms again, trying to make a kiss that lasted forever.

CHAPTER EIGHT

A menacing howl in the distance broke their kiss. Paul would've run if it hadn't been for Mary. Walking quickly, the couple started back to the house. As the howling got closer and louder, they picked up the pace and were running before long.

When they arrived, Jim was standing at the doorway of the cabin, rifle in hand.

"I was just about to go get you lovebirds. Didn't you hear the wolves? It means they're closer than you think. They get desperate with the first snow and come in real close to the houses. I would have suggested you take your rifle, but I didn't want to spoil your first time at the love log."

Jim looked at Mary, as if to read her thoughts.

"I'll take Mary back to the cabin," he said.

"Why don't we all go?" Paul suggested.

"No, it'll only take a minute," Mary said, and they were gone before he could get up.

"What was that all about?" Paul asked when Jim returned to the cabin.

"Oh, she was just telling me how happy she was." Jim smiled, but Paul wasn't sure he trusted it. "What did you do to her out there?" He forced a laugh. "She sure came out of her slump."

Paul didn't like where the conversation was headed. He wasn't sure it was appropriate to talk about what he and Jim's sister did when they were alone.

"The other day, Jim, when we talked? I had something else also on my mind. I noticed Joseph doesn't seem to like me. Did I do something to offend him? I know he didn't like the way Mary and I were dancing at first, but I thought he'd be over it by now, especially in light of present circumstances."

"Joseph is very friendly with the Jacques family across the river. He was the one who set up Mary with Eugene."

The color drained from Paul's face.

"Don't worry, Paul. He'll get over it, eventually."

That night, Paul fell into a deep sleep. He dreamt about Mary. They ran through fields holding hands, the rolled in tall grass and creamy pastel flowers. They were the only people in the world. In paradise.

And then Mary was gone. Wolves were approaching. Big ones, the size of horses. Jumping high enough to snatch birds out of the sky, the wolves growled with blood-drenched fangs as they charged him, eyes ablaze. The hair on their backs stood straight up, ears straight back.

Paul awoke trembling, unsure which wolves were worse, the ones in real life, or those in his dreams.

It was another silent breakfast.

"Well, are you ready for more exercise?" Jim asked when they'd cleared their plates.

Paul shot him a perplexed look.

"Look outside."

During the night another blizzard had passed through; this one left two feet of snow in its wake. Jim and Paul headed down to the shed for the shovels, which they regretted not having left by the front door last night. Before long they were up to their cabin, and as a reward, Mary opened the door to give them hot coffee. The path to Joseph's took no time at all. Joseph must have slept in, because the cabin still seemed too dark and quiet for anyone to be awake inside. It didn't take much time to get from Joseph's to the shed, what Paul had come to think of as the finish line.

As they approached the meat locker, Jim pointed out some paw prints to Paul. Wolves. They cleared the snow away to see what the animals had done. There were prints on top of the cover. They tried to open it, but it was locked. Looking at the rear side, Jim noticed the whole shed was pulled away from the main shed. They got in and pulled some meat out through the opening they made. Paul imagined if he had one of his souped-up trucks, he could have roped the box and pulled it away from the shed. It would be tough with all the ice and snow, but one of his trucks could do it. Large chunks of wood were torn away as though someone had taken an ax to the shed.

"I'll get my father," Jim said, running in the direction of Ray's cabin.

Paul was left there alone with no gun. He thought to go get one, but he didn't want anyone to know he was scared. Instead, he ran after Jim.

At the cabin they explained to Ray what they had found, then went to grab rifles and waited for him to get ready. They went out to the shed and cantilevered it back into place. As the ground was frozen, they had a tough time driving the stakes back in. As a further precaution they strung an electrical cord and light fixture from the main shed so they could keep the area well lit at night. Wolves liked to work in the dark, and the shadows cast by bright lights make them nervous.

"And if that doesn't scare them off, our gunshots will," Ray said.

As they were finishing up, Mary approached to see what the wolves had done. She commented that the wolves seemed more ferocious this year than before. Something must have been stirring them up.

"It's a bad omen," she said.

Paul thought Mary might be implying something. I not only brought them good luck with the moose hunt, Paul assured himself. But the wolves knew I was instrumental in causing them to suffer, and they sensed I was scared of them. Now it's only a matter of time before they get me.

After lunch Paul and Mary went for a walk. Again, they strolled out to the point, but this time Paul brought his rifle and some extra ammunition. As they passed Jims house he made sure Jim knew they were going that way, so he would be listening for gunfire.

He and Mary walked arm in arm, teasing one another. Arriving at the log he put the rifle against the log and sat next to it. Holding each other, their hands began to roam inside each other's coats, feeling the warmth of each other's body. Paul touched her breast again. She sighed into his ear, and her nipples pricked up.

Oh no, he had gotten himself into this again. Not that he didn't like it. He threw snow at her to break the spell. They ended up in a snowball fight, teasing one another, slipping and sliding in the snow, all the while getting further and further away from the log.

Something made Paul freeze. He stopped playing and made a mad dash back to the log, grabbing the rifle.

"You can't be too careful, Mary."

"But—"

"In fact, we should be heading back." He put his arm around her. "Wouldn't want to lose you to the wolves now."

"Mr. Jacques is going to the Norway House in the morning to do some business and pick up a few things," Jean said when Paul and Mary arrived. "He's going in his Bombardier, and he wants you two to join him."

"If it's all right with Mary." Mary smiled. It would be the first time they would be seen in public together, if one counted the river as 'public,' which Mary certainly did.

Early the next morning they headed out across the river. By the time they were out the door, the local kids were already outside, sledding and squealing with glee. Paul had to admit to himself that it looked like fun. But he was too old for that.

All told, there were five of them loading into the Bombardier. Aside from Paul and Mary, Mrs. Jacques wanted to go along with her husband, who was driving. Then there were two Indian women who needed to see the doctor. Paul thought it would have been nice if Jim and Jean could have gone along with them, but there wasn't enough room, especially if they were going to bring back supplies.

Mr. Jacques seemed to take a liking to Paul. Why he didn't know, but he didn't question it. Mary wanted to pick up some things for her wedding. Paul thought it might be nice to get a break from the routine; he was starting to get a little bit of cabin fever.

The mail plane had flown over and dropped a parcel that morning before they left the house. There was a letter from Paul's parents, who had gotten word of the wedding. They wanted to make sure this is what he wanted, and expressed that they were just a little confused, since he'd been close with Alice before he went up to Big Black River. In fact, Alice called wondering about him and when he'd be back. In any case, they told him, they were happy that he was happy, and they wished him luck, adding that they'd like to visit someday soon.

Mary had seen the letter and wondered what it was all about. She didn't get any mail of her own and thought it would be nice if he would share his with her. He told her it was a letter from his parents who wished them both happiness and good luck, and for him to be careful.

"Evidently my Dad told her about the wolves." He was careful not to mention Alice.

Paul told to Mr. Jacques that he had never ridden in one of them before. Mr. Jacques explained how it worked. Paul listened without interrupting, even though he had heard it all from Jim before. They started out down the little hill to the river, followed it out to the lake and turned North.

"How do you know how thick the ice is?"

"It's always thicker near the shore. When you're driving you can feel it under you, kind of bending like a trampoline. Going is always more dangerous than coming home, since it's the first time you're testing the ice. But if we do break through, God forbid, don't panic. The snowmobile floats at least long enough to jump ship. Happened to me once."

Now that he mentioned it, Paul could feel the bowing of the ice underneath him, and decided to remain silent for the rest of the trip so Mr. Jacques could concentrate. As usual, he and Mary were pressed tightly together. Mrs. Jacques looked at Mary inquiringly but didn't speak up. The snowmobile rode along pretty smoothly with the exception of the odd snowdrift.

It took about three hours to get to Norway House. It was a nice community with quite a few stores. There was even a restaurant inside the hotel. Paul invited all of them to have lunch with him and Mary, and afterwards they went their separate ways to shop.

Paul and Mary first found a jewelry store where they bought matching bands. Next they found a flowing white dress for her wedding. They came across a beauty parlor, and though she resisted at first, Paul convinced Mary to go in for a little makeover, just for fun. The ladies were thrilled to have a client; there weren't many new customers. While he waited, Paul walked around until he found a tailor who had the perfect suit, shoes and tie. He headed back to the salon just as Mary was walking out the door. He walked right past her. Wow, there's a real knockout, he thought.

"Paul."

"Mary?" She looked radiant. "Are you sure you want to marry a bum like me? You belong in Hollywood." If he was in love with her before, he was absolutely insane with love now. Now living in California was out of the question; it'd be too tough to hang on to her, with her sharp Indian features and almond skin. She would be too hot a commodity, too exotically beautiful.

Paul steered Mary up the street, ushering her into a furrier's shop.

"Now what?"

"Oh, just a little something I want to get for you." He walked up to the rack where he picked out the fur coat he liked, holding it up so she could try it on. Her eyes grew as big as saucers, and jaw dropped.

"How do you like it? You don't have to take this one. Take your pick."

"Oh no, I like this one. It's lovely."

Paul's heart was racing, not wanting to wake up to the dream that produced such a beautiful woman. He purchased the coat and they headed back to the hotel to meet the others, Mary hanging on his arm the whole way. With some time to spare they shared a slice of pie and some coffee until the others arrived. Mr. and Mrs. Jacques were discomfortingly quiet upon seeing the couple giggling over dessert in the café. Mrs. Jacques's jaw was set, arms folded across her chest.

"You are a very fortunate man, Paul," Mr. Jacques said finally. "We would have been happy to have her as out daughter-in-law. But now all we have is a poor, heartbroken, miserable son. So I hope you two are happy, at least."

Paul, unprepared for this sudden change of heart, set down his coffee.

"Everyone get in the Bombardier," Mr. Jacques said before anyone could get in another word. "We brought you here, so for Ray's sake we'll bring you back."

Where was this coming from all of a sudden? They didn't need to take this from anyone, Paul thought. He was going to

The Innocent Beaver of Big Black River

snap, shout something particularly nasty, or at the very least refuse their ride, but Mary was already piling into the snowmobile with the Indian women, so Paul followed.

Heading back they retraced their tracks. The ride was silent until the Bombardier's engine gave out. Mr. Jacques tried to start it up again, but it was dead. He checked under the dash. Everything looked in order. They had plenty of gas. The problem had to be the engine.

"Can I help?"

"No, I think you've helped us enough for one lifetime."

At this, Paul decided it might be best to leave him be. While Mr. Jacques fought with the engine, Paul hopped out to get some air.

"Take his rifle with you," Mary said as he was leaving. "It was under the seat."

Paul took it and went out the door. Mr. Jacques was back by the engine with the hood open, leaning in to see what was wrong.

If Mr. Jacques had looked down his tracks, he would have seen them coming. They couldn't make very much speed running in the deep snow, but they were smart enough to run in the packed snow made by the Bombardier. They got to Mr. Jacques first. Paul raised the rifle and shot at one, trying to scare them off, but his shot missed and Mr. Jacques went down. He clawed at the reddening snow, hollering hysterically as they tore him apart.

They were on Paul now. He tried to shoot again but they were too close. There was one on the tracks that tried to get him from behind, but he ducked and clubbed it with the rifle, dropping it in the process. He had to get out of there. He somehow made his way backwards up the tracks, kicking at them. He grabbed for a handhold and propelled himself through the door, slamming it in their faces. He held on for dear life.

On the other side of the door, the wolves were howling, calling for reinforcements. On Paul's side it was Mrs. Jacques who was making all the noise. She had something in her hand and was hitting him with it.

"Coward!" She pummeled his back, wailing. Mary took her by the arms and stared at her. Mr. Jacques was gone, and Paul was now their best hope for survival.

"First you steal the love of my son's life, and now you take away my husband! You're a bastard! I want you out, do you hear me? I want this coward out of my husband's car!"

Still clinging to the door of the snowmobile, Paul looked to Mary for sympathy, maybe even advice, but to no avail. A steely anger had washed over her, her eyes like daggers. She had no comfort to give him, no forgiveness.

She took a rope from the toolbox that was under the seat. She tied it to the door handle. She pushed Paul out of the way and tied the other end of the rope to the bottom of the seat, pulling it taut. Now she could sit on the rope and put more pressure on the door. It worked. Before the door would spring open at every snap of the wolves' jaws, but now it was sealed. Now it felt safe.

The wolves started chewing the bottom of the door. Pieces were flying off. Paul couldn't believe his eyes; they were eating through aluminum. Even their own blood didn't stop them as the shredded metal sliced through their skin.

Despite Mary's best efforts Mrs. Jacques was inconsolable, and the two Indian women, paralyzed with fear, weren't much help, either. By this time, Paul had given up; he resigned himself to the storage compartment in the back, where he covered his head with his hands an whimpered. Mrs. Jacques pushed Mary out of the way and was at him again.

"Coward! Coward! Coward!"

The interior vibrated with her screams. Mary instructed the Indian women to sit on the rope while she pulled Mrs. Jacques off of Paul. She slumped into the front passenger seat, still sobbing.

"Oh, my poor husband. My poor husband." Her voice was jagged, exhausted. "And they all thought you were a great wolf hunter. It should have been you out there instead of my husband.

Get out!" She turned her gaze to Mary. "I feel sorry for you. You thought you were getting a real man. Well, there's your real man, hiding behind the seat instead of defending you from a pack of wolves. If we make it out of here alive, you'll be the laughingstock of the whole village."

Light started to peek through the door where the wolves had gotten all the way through. The rope was holding well enough, but the door was unstable. Mary reached for the toolbox again, withdrawing an engine crank. Then, as if she had the luxury to do so, she paused, setting the three-foot crank on the seat next to her, lost in thought. She was brought back to reality by a loud pop made by a rivet bursting. Now the wolves could fit their snouts through the hole. Mary jumped up, grabbed the crank and swung at the wolf's jaw. Blood and teeth flew and the wolf let out a piercing howl. Backing out of the hole, another wolf took its place. Others were climbing all over the bombardier. They looked in the windshield, growling and sneering.

The only thing Paul could bring himself to do was tremble in the storage compartment. As for the girls, he thought, they would've been better off alone. He was hysterical. Listening to what was going on out there, he remembered what happened at the falls and what they did to the meat locker. He saw what they did to poor Mr. Jacques. Eaten alive.

The Indian girls were still in a trance. The aluminum on the door was pulled back far enough for a wolf to put its head through the opening, but the aluminum got snared in its back so it couldn't squeeze in. The women screamed, and Mary swung the crank again, her first blow knocking the wolf unconscious. her second and third blows pulverizing its head. It was a gory sight, blood and brains splattered all over the place. Mary's hair was coming down. She had specks of blood and saliva and brains all over her face.

"If we survive this, Paul," she said, winding up to swing the crank, "I'll do everything in my power to make sure I never see your face again."

She kept swinging the iron until her arms were too tired to lift it. The wolf plugged the opening so the others couldn't come in, which meant they were safe for the time being. But then Mary noticed the other wolves were eating the dead one, removing large chunks of it and trying to get it out of the way. So she took the other end of the rope and made a noose around the wolf's head so they couldn't pull it out. She tied it to the seat frame. However, the wolf's body quickly disappeared, and the head fell into the cab. Another wolf stuck its head in the opening to see if it could come in.

Mrs. Jacques, seeing that Mary was too tired to swing the crank, and now thinking Paul too much a coward to take the reins, she picked up the iron and took a hard crack at the wolf that was now coming through the hole. It ducked out of the way, and the crank struck the side of the door opening, flipping like a wet fish out of her hands.

Now their only weapon lay on the track outside the door. With the end of the rope, Mary tried to snatch the iron crank, but a wolf grabbed it and began to tug against her weight. Another wolf charged the opening and got its head and one leg through. Mary kicked at it from the top, stomping its head with her boot, which the wolf caught in its jaws, refusing to let go.

Now she started screaming. Her screams were so loud that she couldn't hear Paul's own shouts of terror. Then, seemingly by magic, the wolf went limp. Someone had shot it.

Only Mary saw what happened. The other wolves stood, looking off at something coming in the distance before running off. It was all over. She went over to where Paul was hiding, looking down on him with pity.

"You know, Paul, I really loved you. I was afraid you would come into my life and I was going to lose you because I wouldn't be good enough for you, being a half breed and a cousin of all things. I loved you so much it hurt, and there were so many night I went to bed crying because I wanted you so bad. I thought my wishes all came true, but now I see you as you really are.

Everyone thinks of you as a hero, but Mrs. Jacques is right. You're nothing but a coward."

She took off the ring and threw it at him; then she turned, grabbed the package with the dress, and shredded her gown.

CHAPTER NINE

They had been stuck there for about two hours before Jim and the other men had come to the rescue. When they hadn't shown up at the factory, Jim and the rest knew something was wrong, so they cranked up their snowmobiles and went searching. All they needed to do was follow the tracks. After they made sure the Bombardier was no longer under siege, the men ran down the rest of the pack, killing them all.

Removing the wolf from the door, Jim pulled to open it. He hollered for them to untie the rope. Mary jumped out, grabbed him around the neck and wouldn't let go. He looked around to check if everyone was all right. Mary still had her arms around his neck, her face buried in his neck. All was quiet now, except for Mary's childlike crying.

"Jim," Mrs. Jacques cried. "Jim, he—he killed my husband!"

Paul, still in the storage compartment, thought this might be his chance to escape out the door. He didn't even see Jim standing there and almost bowled him over as he slipped on the tracks and fell to the snow.

"Keep her away from me! Keep her away!"

Seeing everyone was okay, Jim went to Paul and walked him over to his snowmobile, then sat him on the back of it.

"Okay, what happened?"

Paul told him the engine had quit when they were attacked by a pack of wolves. He tried to do as much as he could, but they were just too much for him. He was lucky to get inside, but Mrs. Jacques drove him out of his mind. She hated him for taking Mary away from her son. Everything was fine on the way there, but when they saw how beautiful Mary was, after all he'd bought for her, they went out of their minds. Then the wolves attacked and her husband, who didn't want his help, went out to see what was wrong. That's when they hit. He tried to help him but it was too late.

"Now can you just leave me alone? Mary and I are through, and I want to go home."

The other men returned, wolf carcasses strapped to the backs of their snowmobiles. Eugene was among them. When he saw what was left of his father, he fell to his knees, buried his face in his hands and moaned.

Paul didn't know what to say. Instead he just looked at the ice, trying to hide the tears.

"I don't blame you, Paul."

Paul looked up.

"What?"

"This country is hard, and we have to accept what it gives to us."

Paul had fallen from hero to pariah in the span of less than three hours. Upon arriving back at Jims house, Paul collected his belongings and spent the rest of the evening alone. After everyone retired he crawled into his sleeping bag and tried to get some sleep. He was exhausted.

He awoke yelling at the top of his lungs, with Jim and Jean leaning over him, shaking him. He didn't know what they were doing there. Someone came in the door. It was Ray, and behind him was Mary. Paul had been screaming loud enough to wake everyone, even those who'd been sleeping at the other cabin.

Jean got him a hot cup of coffee. Mary didn't say a word. She turned around and went back. Ray and Jim sat there and looked at one another.

"You're sending him home like this?" Ray asked.

"What can I do?"

The next morning after Paul left, Mary walked across the iced-over river. She went to the garage that housed the Bombardier. With a flashlight she looked behind the rear seat; she was searching for her rings and the fur. She found neither. The Bombardier was swept clean. It dawned on her that the old lady Jacques must have them. She went to the house and knocked on the door. Mrs. Jacques's muffled voice told her to come in. As she entered she sat at the table.

"I've come for my Fur and rings and I'm not leaving without them."

The old lady looked surprised and denied having them.

"The only ones who access to them were you and Eugene. The Indian girls couldn't know where they were. And Eugene wouldn't do such a thing. They were no good to him, unless he wanted to sell them. So if you don't mind, please get them for me."

She had the old lady cornered, but the old lady just sat there with a stubborn look.

"If you don't give them to me," Mary continued, "The whole area will know what you've done, and I'll tell the mounted police you stole from me."

Mrs. Jacques got up and went into the bedroom; she came out with Mary's things.

"I deserve these. Paul bought them and he didn't save my husband from the wolves." Eugene came out from his bedroom and said to his mother.

"Let her have them. He bought them for her, not you. If I had a chance to marry Mary I've lost it. Thanks, Ma."

Mary returned to the other side of the river with her belongings. After she entered the cabin her father asked where all the fancy items had come from.

"Paul bought them for me, and I'm keeping them," she said, and went into her bedroom.

The next day the plane landed out on the point and picked him up. No one saw him off. He just walked out to the point, got on the plane, and he was gone. He didn't blame them. He just hoped he didn't cause them too much grief. He was afraid this would happen. He was sensitive, sure, but he wasn't a coward. He had been a soldier in the war, and that never fazed him. It had to be something else. Joseph must be doing a jig by now, he thought. He would patch things up between Mary and the Jacques kid, and he would be the hero. Paul had a dream that he would fit in here, but that was a mistake. As for Mary and Jim, he would remember them always. Who knows, maybe he would see them again someday, but he wouldn't hold his breath.

The plane landed in Selkirk in about an hour. He got a ride to Rose and Pete's. Though they were clearly puzzled, Paul chose not to explain himself, and instead brushed the snow off the windshield of his truck, got in and turned the key in the ignition. It still started. He smiled. at least his truck hadn't let him down. He stood there, letting it worm up for a while, then turned to Pete.

"How much do I owe you? For watching the car, and for me staying with you before?"

Pete's expression changed to that of disgust, and he turned to go back in the house.

Defeated again, Paul figured Pete was about his size, so he left his suitcase full of clothes for him. It was the only thanks he could think of.

It was about ten in the morning. He headed south, crossing the border into the states, then picked up Route 66. The roads were clean and dry. But it did nothing to perk his spirits or change his situation. He was still going home a failure. Everything had been going so well, too. He had let fear in for an instant, and it had consumed him, destroyed his future.

When he got home he wouldn't say anything to his parents about what happened. Hopefully they wouldn't ask. If they did, he wouldn't mention that day in the Bombardier, would say instead that he was only looking out for himself. Like they told him.

Yes, that was it. That life up there just wasn't for him. It just took a while for him to find that out.

It was a long trip to make alone. He scanned the sides of the highways for cops, slowing as he passed and speeding back up as soon as he was out of their sightline. Darkness fell, and he was making good time, but was getting tired. It must be the stress, he thought. Paul caught himself nodding off and opened the window to let the fresh air blow in his face. He drove on and started nodding again. This was dangerous. He slapped himself in the face. That woke him a little, but it wouldn't last.

Entering a small town, he found a motel with a vacancy light on. He pulled in and went up to the office, ringing the bell as he walked through the door. No one came out. He rang it again and waited, but still no one came. He turned and reached for the doorknob

"Can I help you?" An old man stood now stood at the desk.

"I'd like a room."

"Just you?"

"Right."

"That'll be twenty."

"How about eighteen?"

The old man squinted at him.

"Only because it's the last vacancy."

The room was right next to the office. The outside light stayed on all night, so he could see his truck. It wasn't the best motel,

The Innocent Beaver of Big Black River

but he had a solid mattress to sleep in. He stripped down, took a shower and jumped into bed.

At about four in the morning he started dreaming. They came at him from all directions. Mouths open, saliva dripping. The glistening fangs were three inches long. They were charging, but when they got about a foot from him, they disappeared. It happened over and over, round after round of wolf packs. He was fighting them off, kicking and screaming.

"For Christ's sakes knock it off!" Someone was yelling on the other side of the wall, and it woke Paul from his nightmare.

He was sopping wet, so he got up and took another shower. He stood there soaking until the water turned cold. He dried off, dressed and drove off. As he drove the engine sputtered so he switched in a new tank. He had two s left before he had to buy gas. After a couple hours, hunger began to get the best of his stomach. He pulled into the next truck stop he saw and ate a full stack of pancakes with bacon and coffee. Earlier he'd found Dad's thermos and now had it filled.

After that, he ate while he drove. On his C.B., Paul chatted with the truckers, mostly listening. As usual, they criticized the cars on the road; they had endless complaints about the average person's ineptitude when it came to driving. Finally, Paul got tired of it and decided to have some fun.

"This is the Allied Van Lines truck. You know what they should do? They should kick all the cars off the road, then we wouldn't have to worry about them getting in our way. We could make better time and have fewer accidents. We'd have it made."

"They don't know what we go through, driving day and night on all kinds of roads in all kinds of weather. Our rigs are paper boxes, cabs are made of aluminum. With the weight we carry, it's a big risk to drive one of these things. If we could only talk to them, they would have more respect for the danger and drive accordingly."

"I hear ya loud and clear," Paul said. "When do we start?"

Truckers cut in, cheering Paul, who for the first time in a while was starting to feel a bit more like the hero he was purported to be. The truckers carried on their banter without him, and Paul listened contentedly; it kept him awake and in good spirits. He was heading home.

There was a full moon out, and it seemed to follow Paul as he drove. He thought about the wonderful time he'd had before it all ended so horribly. They had done everything for him. Provided for him, loaned him their own cloths to keep warm, showered him with love and respect. Protected him from danger. Even fell in love with him and wanted to marry him.

What had Mary wanted? What did she want now? Could it have been that she was looking for a way to get out of there? But why? It was beautiful there, except in the winter. Maybe she wanted the bright lights and excitement of the city. Or maybe it was real love.

He pulled into his Mom and Dads driveway. The look of the house, the driveway, that safe feeling brought tears to his eyes. He had been through a lot and felt sorry for himself

Ok, Paul, get a hold of yourself, you can't break down now. You have to act like everything is just fine. That you had a good time. The marriage thing just didn't work out.

His Dad came out first, with Mom right behind him.

"We didn't expect you."

"What happened?"

"Glad to have you home."

"Yes, yes. Come in, we were just sitting down to eat."

"Unload your stuff later. Tell us all about the trip."

Paul wasn't sure he was up for the interrogation. Briefly he considered lying, but he'd never been dishonest with his parents before. So he started by explaining how well he was treated, how much he enjoyed hunting moose with Jim.

"Stop beating around the bush, Paul. I was there for all that, and I already told your mother that part. We want to know the rest."

"Mary, you mean?"

"Of course, Mary! What the heck are you doing here if you're getting hitched?" Dad asked.

"As for Mary, well…" How to say this? "Mom, Dad, it just didn't work out. I couldn't adjust to that way of life. I'm guess I'm just a city boy at heart."

Paul unloaded his truck with help from Dad. They chatted while they worked. He said he didn't receive any mail from up there, which was a relief to Paul. Now he had to settle down and get back to finding a job and a place to stay. He sensed there was something his Dad wanted to say but was holding back.

Night fell, and Dad called Paul into the kitchen to give him a few shots of whiskey.

"It'll help you sleep."

It didn't work. No sooner had Paul's head hit the pillow than he could see the wolves, fiercer than ever, racing toward him, surrounding him. He tried to run but couldn't pick up his feet. He tried to fight them off. He would hit one and it would go flying, but there were too many. All at once they lunged at his throat, tearing his flesh from his bone, utterly devouring him alive. He watched his blood spilling, welling up around him. Wolves were pulling at his shoulders, shaking him. Then people were speaking. Someone said pour some water on him. We've got to stop this.

"He's hallucinating. Call 911." It was Dad.

"What's going on? It's not time to get up yet."

"Nightmares, Paul," Mom said. "You were having nightmares."

"He can't go on like this," Dad said.

Going back into Paul's bedroom he sat on the foot of the bed. Mother was there with a warm glass of milk.

"Let's turn out the lights and try to get some sleep, huh?" Dad said.

Paul felt five years old again. He didn't dare let himself fall asleep. Once the sun rose, he went directly into the bathroom, soaked his face in ice-cold water, then went into the kitchen, forcing himself to laugh.

"Guess I gave you both a pretty good scare last night. Must have been the long drive. Sorry about that. What's for breakfast, Mom? I'm famished."

The food smelt good but he didn't have an appetite. He knew not eating would be suspicious, so he shoveled as much as he could into his mouth.

"Before you run off to wherever it is you intend to go, would you mind doing something for me?"

"What's that, Dad?"

"I need you to give my car a tune-up. A good one."

"But—"

"That is, if you don't mind."

Well, maybe he could do it real fast and still get away.

"Great. Thanks, son. You go on ahead and start pulling her apart while I go get you some supplies."

They backed the car into the garage just at the door opening. Digging out the tools, Paul went to work.

Without any new parts, Paul had nothing left to do until Dad arrived.

"Mom, where'd he go? He should be back by now. I have other things to do, you know, I could've walked and gotten back here faster."

He walked to the back of the property behind the garage. It was where his boat was kept. Removing the cover, he checked it over. Everything looked to be in working order, just as he left it. Maybe I should be out on a lake somewhere, he thought, sun beating on my back, free as all the fish in the sea.

The Innocent Beaver of Big Black River

He heard Dad drive up, so he went back around to greet him.

"I'm not going to ask where you went, I only want you to know that now it's going to be late by the time I get done with your car."

"Okay. No hurry. Stay another evening with us. I stopped by the store and bought us some nice steaks. Your mother is preparing them as we speak."

"But, the car—"

"Forget the car. We can finish it tomorrow."

Using the new parts, he put the engine back together and was fine-tuning it when Mom called him in to eat. He backed the car up and closed the garage door. When he sat down, his food was already on the table, and the steaks were perfect. Mom washed the dishes before serving dessert. It was now early evening and Paul was getting fidgety.

"Where are you going this hour? Relax. Anyway where would you stay tonight if you left? In some cheap motel, when you can be sleeping here? I won't hear of it . Tomorrow we'll test the car, then you can go."

Paul knew there wasn't anything he could do.

"So, still thinking of starting your own garage?"

"Who said anything about that?" The garage seemed like lifetimes ago.

"A friend of yours called here and wanted to make sure you called him back. Something about partnership for a new garage."

"Did he leave his name?"

"Peterson, I think. That sound right?"

"Don Peterson?"

"Yeah, that's it."

Paul nearly choked on his food.

"But before you start a partnership, make sure you think things through. Most times it's better to go it alone. I know you can afford it, so why carry some one else?"

This discussion kept Paul's mind busy, so when he went to bed he was thinking about his shop. But before long he could see them coming again, from far off, racing through the trees. Paul was ready for them this time. He had two six-shooters, one on each hip, with extra shells in his gun belt. Two bandoleers loaded with shotgun shells. Two automatic shotguns, one slung over each shoulder. Two large bowie knives, one in front and one under his arm.

He struggled to a spot on top of a rock ledge that was Steep on one side and sloping on the other. He shot again and again; they were accurate. The wolves were going down, making a large, blood-soaked pile. He was winning, slaughtering them. He would teach them to mess with him. Next he started with his shotgun, blazing away . The pile got bigger and bigger. He still wondered where they all came from. Now the pistols. One in each hand. It was Custer's Last Stand. First this one. Then that one. Then two at a time. The pile grew. The pistols were empty. Click click click click click. He had no time to reload.

Dropping the pistols, Paul pulled out both bowie knives. Now he was slashing, thrusting, stabbing. Wolves fell at his feet. He was standing on them, almost losing his balance.

"Take that!"

He was holding his own for now, but he wouldn't last forever. He wasn't going to give up, though. He would survive, even if it was impossible. He stumbled over a dead wolf and dropped a knife as two wolves lunged, one of them biting right into his arm. Flailing, Paul tried to slit its throat, but it was thrashing and he couldn't get a clean thrust with the knife. The muscles in his arm were cut up pretty bad, and the bone was shattered. Useless.

The wolf let go and stood in front of him. Mouth wide open, teeth bloody and dripping, the wolf grabbed Paul's other arm with such force that he dropped the only knife he had left. The wolf jerked at his arm and stripped the muscles down to the white bone. Now it started to eat him, piece by piece. They were now doing it to him now, just like they'd meant to all along.

One wolf took him by the throat, squeezing harder and harder, sinking its teeth in. Paul was done for.

"Please, finish it. Don't let me suffer like this."

His parents heard him grunting and cursing and making all sorts of terrifying sounds.

"My arm! Ohhh, my arm."

He was thrashing around without moving his arms. Dad grabbed him by the shoulders and held him still. As Paul awoke he could hear him.

"Paul. Paul, take it easy. It'll be all right. Calm down."

CHAPTER TEN

"Now, I'm not going to take no for an answer on what I'm about to tell you," Dad said to Paul over breakfast the next morning. "I realized something must've happened up north that you don't want to talk about. That's ok if you don't want to tell me, but you have to tell someone. So I made an appointment with my friend. He's a psychiatrist."

Paul dropped his spoon.

"Finish up and get ready, or we'll be late."

Paul was going to interrupt, but his father put up his hand.

"You heard what I said, now let's get at it." Dad hadn't talked to him like that for a long time. Paul conceded.

The doctor's name was Conrad Cox. He had a nice office in the upscale part of town.

"Come on in and sit down," he said. "Now before we start, is it alright if your dad sits over there in the corner and listens in?"

Paul didn't think that was right.

"He won't say a word. Now what I want you to do is start from the beginning. Tell me everything that happened to you. Don't leave anything out, ok? Ok, I'm just going to press this button and…Start." He pushed a button on his recorder. Paul sat back in the recliner.

First Paul gave his age and what he did for a living, then he told the doctor how he felt about himself. As he did this, the doctor made notes on a pad, occasionally looking down at his watch. Paul started recounting his trip to Canada. When he was through he mentioned that he now has these horrible nightmares, and that they were getting worse. He wanted to get on with his life but he couldn't. Not like this.

"Do you think you can help me?"

The doctor was silent for a while.

"You've had an exciting time for yourself. Have you ever had or experienced a fear like this before?"

"I was in the service. I hunt and fish. I do all kinds of things that could make a person afraid, but fear never bothered me until now."

"I think your fear started when you were in the front of the canoe and confronted that beaver. You would have gotten over it if nothing else had happened to you, but then there were the wolves. You held it in, not wanting others to know you had the fear in you. If you fought the fear, chances are you'd be all right. Now you have to get it out of your head. Let it go.

"Then there's the girl. She wanted you and wouldn't take no for an answer. She pursued you knowing you were her cousin, and knew you couldn't say no, because you didn't want to cause trouble between them and your Dad. You didn't want to hurt her, and you didn't want them to know you developed this fear that you might not be the hero they thought you were."

Paul sat up. He turned to look at Dad, who was doing anything to avoid Paul's gaze. Dr. Cox continued.

"It's best that this is coming out now, at an age that you can control it. Now we have to get it out of your head. We are going to start with talking about it. Getting it out on the table, so to speak. In the meantime, I'm going to prescribe a tranquilizer so you can get some sleep. We may even try hypnoses at some point. In any case, we'll cure you."

On the way home they stopped and got the prescription filled.

"You really have been through a lot. And you need a lot of help, so this is what I'm going to propose. Right now you don't have a place to stay, so you stay with us as long as it takes. Second, you don't have a job. We have our little side deals, so it's not like you'll be broke. If you feel you want to keep busy you can maybe get a job close by. But whatever happens, you stay with us until you're well, you hear?"

When they pulled into the driveway, Dad and Paul could see Alice inside talking to Mom. They looked at one another. The curtain in the window moved as the two women parted it to see who had arrived.

"I have to run down to the corner, Dad. I, uh, forgot something."

"Now cut that out, Paul. You can't keep running away from her. You have to see her sooner or later. Either you want to be with her or you don't."

"But I was unfaithful. I almost married someone else."

"You can either tell her now, or later, or not tell her at all. What you did didn't work out, anyway. So what's the problem? Maybe it took all this to straighten you out, so you can get on with your life."

Paul sat in the idling cab with his father for a moment. Then he stepped out of the car.

Alice ran to him and hugged him when he walked through the front door.

"I'm glad you are back. I missed you terribly. Why didn't you write? No, forget I said that. I'm just glad your home."

They walked into the living room and sat together on the sofa. She put her arms around his neck.

"I haven't seen anyone since you left and won't see anyone else as long as you want me." Paul tried to interrupt but she put her finger on his lips and continued. "That evening you called, and we got into the fight? It was Mark who was at my house. He was over doing odd jobs for me. So say you're sorry, and give me a kiss."

They kissed as though they'd never been apart.

At the lunch table they mostly made small conversation. Paul and Alice kept giggling to each other.

"Your mom said you were at the doctor. What happened?" Alice asked.

"Oh." Paul turned to his father. "Should I tell them, Dad?"

Dad nodded. Paul explained his situation, the trauma he went through and the pills the doctor had prescribed. When he was through, Alice hugged him first, then Mom. They told him it would be okay.

Paul was going to relax for a few days, then look for a job locally. He started making plans with Alice again as their relationship healed. However, Paul felt as though his heart had stopped healing. The awful feeling was returning.

He went back to the doctor, who lately Paul thought was more interested in hearing the stories than actually doing anything about his problem.

"I'm not getting any better."

"Are you taking your pills? When you feel you need a refill, let me know."

At the next session, the doctor hypnotized him. When it was through, Paul couldn't remember anything.

"You made progress," the doctor told him. But he didn't feel any different, and it had been six months.

Starting the next day, Paul stopped taking his pills. Monday night he was all right and thought he had it licked. But by Tuesday night, the wolf sat there on its haunches, glaring at him. It didn't move, and it wouldn't go away, just sat there licking its chops, opening its mouth, baring its teeth. Paul slept through this, twisting and turning. But at least he slept.

He awoke the next morning unable to shake the dream from his thoughts. Maybe this was as good as it would get. Maybe he wouldn't get any better. Could he live with this? He thought he might be able to.

By Thursday night, Paul's Dad knew he stopped taking his pills, so he was praying for him. About three in the morning it started. The wolves were walking instead of running. Paul tried to ease away from them, but they followed him. He walked faster, but they now closed the distance. Snow was all around them. He slipped and slid, had a hard time getting anywhere. He faltered, got up quickly; he didn't want them to catch him defenseless, on the ground. He slid down a hill into a gully where he picked up a dead branch and swung it at them as they came. He hit one and the branch broke.

Now they had him. They had him down. One was chewing on his right leg. Another on the left. He was trying to kick them off but another was eating his right arm. He lost his right leg. Two wolves were fighting over it. Two more were trying to take his left leg off. Where was his right arm? Gone.

Suddenly Paul awoke, sopping.

"We were trying to hold you down. I think this is the worst one you've had so far. I noticed the neighbors put their kitchen lights on."

The next day Paul called the doctor. He didn't have an appointment but insisted on seeing him anyway.

"I didn't take my pills, to see what would happen. Monday night was bearable. Tuesday night was the worst I ever had. Your treatment isn't actually fixing anything, not permanently."

The doctor raised his hand, knowing Paul was upset.

"Look, you're like a child that thinks there's a monster under the bed. The only way to convince the child is to turn on the light and look."

Paul stood outside the doctor's office. He was dumbfounded. Go back up there, he thought. Give them a piece of your mind. No, maybe he's right. Maybe if I'd let it all out when it happened, I wouldn't be like this right now. It's like a rollercoaster. You scream. Everyone does. You get it out of your system. I held it in to show them I wasn't afraid, and all this time I was burying it in my mind. He's right, I have to go back. And I have to do it by myself.

He walked back into the office; the doctor, who was standing near the receptionist, tried to dart back into an exam room.

"Wait, no," Paul said. "I want to thank you. I think you fixed me, after all."

"What'd the doctor say?" Mom asked when Paul arrived.

"I don't know if the doctor meant to or not, but I think he solved my problem. I have to go back up there and face my problem head-on. The sooner the better."

His parents were stunned into silence.

"I have to see Alice."

He went to the phone and called her at work, arranging to have dinner with her later that evening. The rest of the day he spent filling the truck with gas and making sure it was in good enough condition for the trip. Then he got to work on the boat. He put in provisions, his rifle, ammo and camping gear. Paul hauled the boat out into the driveway so he could hook it up to his truck. Afterwards, he went to his room and put some clothes in a duffel bag, making sure to pack his warmest leather coat; it would be cold out on the lake. He asked Mom if she could pack him a lunch and if he could take Dad's thermos for coffee.

"You're not leaving right this second, are you?"

"No," he answered. "Not until tomorrow morning."

He looked around the house for anything else he might need, scooping up a medicine kit as he went along. He thought about taking the pistol, but he didn't want to worry about taking it across the border, since the license for it wasn't his. Going out to the garage, Paul worked his knife on the stone. It was sharp already, but he wanted to put a fine edge on it. When he finished, Paul was sure it could slice through anything.

Alice drove up. He walked to the back door of the house and told his Mom they would be gone for a while. He went to her car and got in beside her.

"Let's go to our favorite park."

"Why did you want to see me on such a short notice?"

"I'll tell you when we get there."

They parked close to the spot where they always sat.

"Paul, I think I know what this is all about, and before you tell me, I have something to say."

"No, Ali—"

"I love you, and I know that you love me. We've had our problems in the past, but we resolved them. I can't go on like this loving you and not knowing if there is a chance for us. Your wanting to see me like this scares me. If you are going to say goodbye, then get it over with."

Paul turned her so he could look into her eyes. She wasn't crying, exactly.

"I know I've been selfish in the past, but this has nothing to do with that. You've always been there for me when I needed you. Yes, we should be together. But things have come up that I have to take care of. My doctor told me today that the only way I'm going to defeat my demons is to face them. I have got to go back up north and somehow get this out of my head. I'm going to leave tomorrow morning. I don't know when I'll be getting back, or if I'll get back at all. I wanted to tell you before I gave you this." He reached into his pocket and took out an engagement ring. He had purchased it on the way home from the doctor. "I'm asking you to marry me, but there's a hitch."

"What?"

"You have to wait 'til I get back. I'm giving this to you now for you to decide. You don't have to answer now. I just didn't want to leave before you knew my intentions."

He made like he was going to get up, but she put her hand on his arm and looked in his eyes. She put on the ring. Alice held up her hand and smiled.

The Innocent Beaver of Big Black River

"I—" Alice cleared her throat. "I will go anywhere you go and would do anything you want me to do. I'm willing to fight your problem with you, Paul. I've always been willing. But I'll also love you just as you are." She kissed him. "Now let's run home and tell your parents. This calls for a celebration."

They bought a bottle of champagne on there way home. Paul had the bottle in his hands as they walked through the door, and immediately his parents knew what was up. Paul set the champagne on the table.

"I have something to tell you. I asked Alice to marry me, and she accepted."

Dad was all smiles and tears. They kissed and hugged and toasted the bride- and groom-to-be.

"To a long, happy, and healthy marriage," Mom said.

"With many grand children," Dad said.

After the brief celebration, Alice had to go home. It was a workday tomorrow, and her boss was good enough to let her get off early today, so she didn't want to be tired in the morning. She didn't want to seem disrespectful. Paul walked her out to her car.

"Alice, I'll be gone for a while. I don't know how long, and I won't be able to write, but I want you to know that I'll be thinking of you every day. Not just of you, of us."

She started crying.

"Please come back to me. I love you so much, and now that I have you, I don't want to lose you."

"And you know I love you, too. I'll make it all work out right. You'll see. And remember, honey, pray for me."

She reached into her glove compartment and pulled out a piece of red ribbon.

"Wear this. It's supposed to ward off evil spirits."

After kissing long and hard, she left. Paul turned and entered the house. Mom and Dad were already sitting and waiting for him to have coffee and cake. his Dad spoke." I know you've made up your mind to go. I want to go with you. When I needed you to go with me, you were there. Now you need me."

Paul looked at him sharply, not wanting to have to tell him no outright. Thankfully, Dad understood.

"Listen," Paul said. "The truck will probably be at Pete's, the boat at Ray's. So if I don't come back—"

Mom gasped.

"What do you mean, don't come back?" Dad asked.

"Come on, Dad, you saw how it was out there." They were all silent for a moment. Mom was trying not to cry. "Well, if I don't come back, my remains will probably disappear, so you won't have to concern yourselves with that."

"Paul, don't say things like that," Mom said through tears. "You know you are coming back."

"There is one other thing. Please pray for me, because I know I'm going to need it."

He didn't take a pill that night, so again he dreamt of wolves. Mom slipped out of bed and sat there consoling him until morning. She got a wet cloth and wiped his face.

When he awoke, he saw her sitting there. He knew she'd been there all night, watching over him. He had a lump in his throat. He had put them through a lot since he'd come home from Big Black River. He would make it up to them some day. He touched her arm.

"I'll make you a good breakfast while you clean up your things."

"I have something here I want you to take with you," Dad said, handing him the shotgun. Paul was just loading the last of his things after breakfast. "Works like a charm. I'm also giving you some buckshot. You hit them with this, and they won't get up."

"But that's your favorite. It can't be replaced."

"I could lose a lot more. I insist."

Hugging one last time, Mom made Paul promise to come back safe. He would. His Dad shook his hand, and then they embraced.

"Please be careful. Don't do anything drastic. And if you need me for anything, you call, and I'll be there. Drive safe. Stop and rest. I'm thinking you should be back in about a week, so don't disappoint me. Have a good trip, son."

Paul opened the boat cover and put the shotgun and shells in a safe place. He rechecked all his hookups. He was ready.

"Remember. Pray for me," he said, pulling out of the driveway and onto the road.

CHAPTER ELEVEN

He headed north at eight o'clock, planning to travel the same route he traveled coming home. He made good time to Denver. In two days he crossed the border. The border guard walked around his rig, wished him luck with his fishing, and waved him through. He buzzed through Winnipeg and pulled into Rose and Pete's yard in Selkirk.

No one was particularly impressed with Paul this time around, even though he had a flashy new boat in tow. The group of people who'd rushed out the door just as quickly returned inside. Pete was the last to come out.

"I need help," Paul said. Maybe it was the way he said it, but Pete came up to him and hugged him.

"What can I do for you?" He didn't want their sympathy so all he told them was that he was going back up to cure himself of something that had been bothering him. Pete looked at Paul.

You can put your truck in the same spot as before and the trailer along side of it."

"Could you see me off at the dock and bring the truck and trailer back here? The trailer pushes real easy."

"You mean you trust me with your rig?"

"You bet."

The Innocent Beaver of Big Black River

Paul ran in to say goodbye to Rose, then he and Pete were off to the dock.

When they got to the river, Pete helped Paul unload the boat.

"You know, you ought to be careful on the lake with this boat. It's shallow water, you're likely to lose a prop."

Paul smiled and showed him the back. There was no propeller. Paul explained it was a jet boat; it could still run in only three inches of water. The boat carried fifty gallons of gas and could go about fifty-five miles per hour. He should get up to the river in about only a couple hours.

Pete hugged Paul again and said good luck.

Paul started the engine, which purred. Pete stood there watching him go and waved as he got up to speed. Paul didn't worry about his truck or trailer

Paul ran the river slow enough not to make large waves. People watched as he went by; some waved. He wondered if it was at him or the boat, or both. He didn't have to watch the markers as he went by because he didn't draw that much water. When he found a straightaway he set his steering and worked at putting up the windshield and convertible top. He checked everything to make sure everything was tied down so nothing would come loose as he accelerated.

There was a little roll to the water when he got to the lake, but with a V-shaped front and a flat rear bottom, the ride was smooth. He ate some sandwiches and cookies with the coffee from Dad's thermos. When he was finished, he sat back in his comfortable chair and let her run by herself. He passed other boats coming and going. They waved and saluted hello. He looked good on the water.

Way off in the distance he saw the back of a steamer. Paul kept his eye on it. Could it be? Who else could it be? He slowed down and as he went by he laid on his horn and waved. He hoped the captain recognized him. In any case, the ship signaled with a loud blast on it horn. This made Paul feel good.

He went back to his cruising speed and before long he was at Big Black River. He slowed her down a bit and turned into the mouth. Now he throttled back and ran the river to Ray's dock. There was no room to tie up so he tied to one of the other boats, then walked across it and up the path to the cabin.

"Where do you think you're going?" Paul stopped to look. It was Joseph, and he was standing next to Ray's cabin.

"Hello."

"What do you want?"

"I want to talk to Jim."

"Jim's not here. He won't be back until tomorrow."

"Maybe I can talk to you, then. Please. You know I wouldn't ask you unless I had to."

"Fine, you can talk, and then you can take your fancy boat and get out of here."

"I want to go back. I want to rent a canoe and paddle. I'll give you thirty dollars for it, and I'll return it when I'm through. And I'd like to tie my boat up to Jim's dock while I'm gone, too. I'll pay him for his trouble when I get back. And if I don't get back he can work it out with my Dad. After this, I promise I'll never bother any of you ever again."

Paul was silent for a while. He realized he was begging.

"Let him have my canoe," Ray called from inside. "And I don't want any of his money. You tie his boat up to the other side of the dock."

Paul wasn't sure what to say, so instead he just did as he was told, packing up the most essential supplies in a bag that would fit in Ray's little boat. Joseph came around the corner with the canoe. Once he was loaded, he pulled away from the dock, waving his hand.

"Thank you."

Joseph didn't respond.

Immediately, Paul almost flipped the canoe over. He had too much weight on one side. The river was pulling him towards the lake. He straightened out his load, positioned himself in his seat and started paddling. All the while Joseph stood there watching him. The current took him down as far as the factory. He turned the canoe around and now was paddling back by Joseph again. As he went by he nodded, then kept going up the river.

He started remembering what Jim taught him about canoeing, and he found it wasn't as hard as he remembered. He didn't have to worry about making any noise, just kept it going in the right direction. He was starting to feel like a pro. The canoe was old but in good condition, and it handled well. He found that if he stayed close to shore, he could make better headway.

Now that he was under way, he thought about the people standing on the bank watching him. Maybe someone told them there was a city boy out on the river. He thought he saw Mary in the group, but he couldn't be sure.

He had to concentrate on what he was doing. He wanted it to look like he had been doing it for a long time. Around the bend was high brush and as he came around it, a bear was practically on top of him. He surprised it as much as it surprised him. It made like it was going to attack the canoe. Quickly, Paul picked up the shotgun and let go a blast, just to scare it off. The bear fell into the water, then reared up and ran off.

Soon he was coming up to the waterfalls. He pulled up to the landing, took a rope in hand, got out and tied the canoe to a tree. He made sure that it was real secure; Paul couldn't bear the thought of losing the canoe. It would be awful, he could see it now. The villagers on the banks, they'd be laughing as the empty canoe floated past.

Now was the time to think. He wouldn't get a second chance. Checking the shotgun to make sure it was loaded and that he had extra shells in his pockets, Paul hauled everything to the top landing. He headed back to get the canoe, which was suddenly looking a lot larger than he remembered. He wondered if he could carry it alone. There wasn't much by way of choice. He slung the shotgun over his shoulder, grabbed the canoe with both hands and flipped it up over his head, backing away from the edge of the river so as not to fall in. This wasn't so bad. He walked to the upper landing, and set it down the same way as he picked it up in the water. He tied it off. He was starting to like this.

Once on his way again, he found a rhythm and began to zip along. He went by the flat rock, where Jim had played the trick. Paul scared up some ducks, and some loons played in the water in front of him as he paddled upstream. Their gurgling soothed him. Up ahead other birds were signaling his coming.

He saw a cow moose and her calf leaving the water and running into the woods. He wanted to go on forever like this. At one point he rounded another bend in the river. As the front of the canoe stuck out into the current, the current took it and swung it around. Now he was going back the way he came. Instead of panicking, Paul aimed the canoe for a sandy beach and put the nose of the canoe into the shore. The current took the canoe and swung it around the right way. He was learning on the job.

Not wanting to get caught on the river in the dark, Paul started digging into it and traveled a lot faster. Passing the spot he and Jim camped the first night, he let out a chuckle and wondered which animal had gotten his supper.

There was the spot where Paul had seen the beaver. A chill ran up his spine.

Finally, he landed where they had dressed the moose the first night. It was a good place to camp with plenty of room. Flat, with lots of trees. He pulled up the canoe, emptied it and turned it over. In a rock pit, he started a fire with branches. It looked like someone had spent the night there before. The rocks were already in a circle. He heated some coffee in a pan and ate a cold supper; he was more interested in setting himself up with a place to sleep. There were four trees about the right distance apart. With his ax he cut some poles about two to three inches in diameter. He

The Innocent Beaver of Big Black River

lashed them as best he could to the four trees, making a square about five feet off the ground, like a lofted bed. It was about four by six, all told. Looking at it he knew it wasn't the best, but it would hold him for the night. He moved a nearby rock to use as a stepstool for his makeshift bunk.

His fire was going out so he put another log on to keep the animals away. There was a little coffee left, so he sat and finished it off. He had on his sheep-lined leather jacket. In the pockets he had extra shells for both the shotgun and the rifle. The rifle wasn't good for close shooting because it had a scope on it, but he thought he could just point it. If he hit a wolf with it, it would blow it apart.

As he sat there he noticed how quiet it was. There wasn't any night sounds. Even the wind was still. Usually you hear owls, moose, and bears. There was nothing. It was almost eerie like something was going to happen. He felt like maybe he made a mistake coming here. This was starting to get to him. He started looking at the edge of the campfire light. He started imagining things were looking at him. Then he got a hold of himself. This is like a kid thinking there's something under the bed. He thought." I've got to keep a clear head if I'm going to survive.

He was getting tired, so he hopped up on the rock and into his improvised bed. He got into his sleeping bag, put the rifle on his left side and the shotgun on his right. Now he waited for sleep to take him. He wondered if he was going to have a nightmare, but thought he had to fight to prevent it. He only knew that providence pushed him in this direction.

Then again, maybe nothing would happen. Then what? If nothing happened, Paul told himself, he would just go back home and take whatever life dished out to him back there.

When he felt the ripping of teeth in his sleeping bag, Paul was not surprised. This is what I came for, he thought.

He had to fight back. From inside, he unzipped his bag, then grabbed his shotgun, jamming the stock against a branch of his bed before swinging the barrel into position and firing. Providence was not done with him yet. The weight of the wolf added to Paul's own weight was enough to snap his perch. He landed on the ground in a sitting position, with his back up against the tree. He was still in his sleeping bag, shotgun still gripped tight in his right hand. He was tangled in the branches.

In the half-dark he saw a wolf coming at him from the left side. He swung the shotgun around, holding the barrel with his left hand, then pointed it at the wolf and pulled the trigger. The shotgun bucked and another wolf was gone. He twisted back to his right as the third one landed on top of him. It lunged at his throat. All he saw was a big mouth with lots of teeth about to finish him. He brought up his left arm to ward off the attack, but instead the wolf took his arm, biting through his jacket. He thought it was going to break the bone. The pain was excruciating. He was about to black out, but he fought to stay conscious.

The shotgun was empty. He didn't know where the rifle was, even though it wouldn't have done him much good. He let out a scream, something like Jim's war call. The next thing he knew he had his knife in his right hand. He was holding the wolf's head up with his left and was pulling the knife across the wolf's throat. He could feel the blood spraying all over him as the creature trembled and twitched, weakening. Flickering. With one last jab he plunged the knife into its chest all the way to the hilt.

He was still in his sleeping bag, and now Paul tried to get out by unzipping it the rest of the way. Something pulled the wolf off of him. He let out another scream and pulled the knife out of the wolf. He was about to strike out with the knife, when he heard a voice.

"It's all over. You killed them all. You're safe now."

It sounded like Jim, but what would Jim be doing here? When Paul was finally able to get out of the sleeping bag, he noticed someone over at the fire, stoking it up. Paul went over to the tree and pulled his gear down. Opening it, he came to the fire with the coffee and put on a pot. The silhouetted man pulled up a log and sat down.

Paul was surprised to find he wasn't shaking or breathing hard anymore. He was as calm as could be. He found his rifle and shotgun and had them by his side.

"You've changed," said the man, now illuminated by the firelight.

"Jim!"

"How come you came here all by yourself? You could have been killed."

"It all started with the beaver."

"The beaver?" Jim leaned in.

"Yeah. I was so scared, not knowing what it was. I could have screamed, but I held it in. Then the wolves. I could be all right as long as I pretended to be, or so I thought. But when we were attacked out on the lake, I did the best I could to fight them off. I really did. After I got home I started having nightmares about wolves. They were driving me insane. Don't you understand? I had to come up here. To face my fears."

"There is something about you, Paul Pauquette, I'll tell you that. What it is, that's a mystery to me. You know, the Indians around here say you're like medicine. You bring the beast here, and they try to destroy you because they fear you. What you did here tonight, they told me you'd do it. I came here because, I don't know, I couldn't or wouldn't believe them. And maybe I thought you needed my help. It could be that your nightmares were the wolves calling you back. I know it's only Indian talk. Hell, after this you'll probably go your way and never come back. But I can say I will always remember you. Now let's clean up this mess you made and get out of here."

When Paul picked up his canoe, he almost dropped it; the pain in his left arm was excruciating. Jim saw him fumbling, but when he saw him managing the canoe, he kept going. Paul wanted to show him he could do it himself. They were standing there, ready to get into their canoes, when off in a distance there was a lone howl.

At the dock, Paul graciously declined Jim's offer of hospitality.

"Actually, for once I'm in a hurry to get back home."

"At least let me bandage your wounds."

"What wounds?"

"You can't see yourself, can you? Wait here."

When he came back, Mary was with him. She had a medicine kit. She daubed at a bad cut on his face and put some stretch bandages on it. But he would have to have it stitched. She made him take off his jacket and put disinfectant on the teeth marks.

"It's a good thing this is a thick jacket," she said.

"I want you to know that I'm sorry."

"So am I."

He was about to leave when he saw Ray coming down the path. Paul got out of the boat. To his surprise, he was not afraid. Ray put his arms around him.

"Tell your Dad I'll never forget him. Or you."

" I never got the chance to thank all of you for everything you did for Dad and me. Me especially."

He climbed back into his boat and started the engine. As he backed out, he looked at them all and waved goodbye. As Jim pushed him off, Paul grabbed his rifle and tossed it to him. Not wanting it to land in the water, Jim made a quick grab for it, which caused Paul to laugh uproariously.

"Think of me when you shoot it."

He headed out to the lake and cruised all the way to Selkirk, where he paid a kid ten dollars to watch his boat, which he tied up to the first empty slip he found. He hoofed it to Pete's house, hoping he would be home.

He knocked on the door, and a few minutes later, Pete appeared in the window. When he saw Paul, his expression changed. He turned around and came out with the keys to the truck, which was covered with a large canvas.

"Your idea?"

Pete nodded. They removed the canvas and put it on the step. Paul started the truck, pulled it around and hooked the trailer onto it, then drove to pick up the boat.

As they pulled up, they noticed a group of people looking at the boat. Paul backed the trailer down the ramp, untied the boat and winched it onto the trailer. He then pulled it out of the water. A well-dressed gentleman approached.

"How much do you want for your rig, just as it stands?"

"Not for sale."

The man saw the condition of Paul's face and decided to walk away.

Paul took a minute to check his truck before the long drive. He had about a tank and a half of gas. Enough to get to the border.

As he let Pete off he ran to the step and put a package there, then ran back to the truck.

"You don't have to do this," Pete said, coming around to the driver's side and taking Paul's hand. "I'm not going to ask how everything turned out up there, but for the look of things, I think it turned out all right.

"Everything is just fine, and I couldn't have done it without your help." With that he drove off, Pete standing there watching him get smaller on the horizon until he turned a corner and was out of sight. Paul buzzed through Winnipeg and entered the same border station, where the same guard was on duty.

"What happened to your face?"

"Cut myself shaving." He laughed. The guard started to lose his sense of humor. "No, I fell. Slipped on a rock. The fish that got away."

"Have a good trip home."

He stopped at a drugstore and bought some bandages. When he stopped at gas stations and restaurants, people stared at him, but he paid the attention no mind. Often on the way he would look in the rearview mirror to find himself bleeding. He wiped away the blood and drove on.

He was getting tired and started dozing off; he stopped at a clean, well-lit motel.

"We're all filled up," said the woman at the desk upon seeing Paul.

Paul pointed at the vacancy sign. She turned it off. As Paul pulled out, he noticed the sign flickering back on in the mirror.

He drove on a ways and came on to another motel.

"I'll pay you a little extra in case I get blood on your pillowcases," he offered.

"You know," the receptionist said, "We'd just rather not get involved in your personal life."

"So you don't mind about my face?"

The receptionist shook her head. She took out a map of the motel and pointed to the square where his room was located.

"Here's the key, sir."

"Thank you."

"You're welcome. Have a nice night. Sleep well."

In the room, he stripped and got in the shower, letting the water spray on his face and arm. It felt good. The towels were soft. He bandaged up his wounds and went to bed.

To his surprise, he slept without dreaming. He awoke to daylight. He stopped at the truck stop and ordered breakfast. In a booth were two Policeman, and when they saw him they both came over. He was expecting trouble because of the state of his face.

"We hear you killed a timber wolf with your bare hands. Is it true?" The cop looked at him. Paul noticed the diners had all stopped eating and were listening in.

"I don't really have time to tell you the whole story, but while I'm eating I'll fill you in." He repeated the story, relishing each

The Innocent Beaver of Big Black River

stab of the knife. Now they believed him, believed he was heroic. He also had an audience, truckers stretching their necks to see the wounds. "Do you have any reason to keep me?"

"No."

"Then no offense, fellas, but I'm not going to let you get in the way of my wonderful mood. Goodbye, and have a nice day." He paid his bill, smiled at the waitress and left.

He still had a long ways to go, so Paul turned on his C.B. to enjoy the gossip. The truckers were talking about him. Some marveled at what he had done. Others didn't believe it, and they argued that they knew how big these wolves were.

He was making good time. A truck pulled in behind him and kept motioning for him to turn on his C.B. Paul ignored him for a long ways, but the truck driver persisted. Paul couldn't get away from him because of the boat. He tried maneuvering with the traffic but that didn't do any good. The trucker was good. He stayed right with him. Paul would get a few cars ahead, but here he would be again, right behind him. Finally, Paul got tired of playing cat and mouse with him and gave in. He turned on his C.B.

"Okay, what do you want, before we kill someone."

"Hey, you handle that rig real well. Truckers put out a call that you're the guy who got the timber wolves. Just wanted to know where you found them."

"Winnipeg."

"In my time off, I go hunting and have shot just about everything grown on this continent, and I can prove it because I had 'em all stuffed. I'll give you my address and you can come see my collection."

Paul didn't know if this was a good idea and thought if he went along with him he would get off the C.B. and leave him alone, so he got back on.

"O.K. I've got a pen and paper. What is it?"

The trucker gave the address and directions from the interstate. Paul cut back in.

"Do you think it's a good idea to give this information over the C.B.?"

"I pity the soul who comes to my place uninvited. Speaking of which, you might want to take down my phone number so you can call ahead."

Paul was now certain this was a man of his word.

"I've got quite a few things in the works so it may be a quite a while, but I will call. Nice talking to you, and just maybe I'll see you on the road again. I gotta go, I'm almost home, but keep your tires on the road and not up in the air. Out."

CHAPTER TWELVE

He wasn't tired so he drove on, holding his speed until he got to the road that led to his parents' house. When he pulled into the driveway, Erney's truck was there. He parked in behind it and got out of the truck.

Both his Mom and Dad burst out the door and ran to him; it was like returning from the war all over again. Dad let Mom hug him.

"Your face, your face, what happened to your face?"

"It doesn't matter now."

He hugged her and kissed her cheek. Dad squeezed in, taking Paul's hand.

"Glad to have you home."

"I'll tell you all about it later, but now I'm famished. Let's go out, and I'll buy you a nice dinner."

"Hey, Paul."

"Erney," Paul called out to his brother, who was now standing in the driveway.

"Your rig is in my way. Get out here and move it."

Paul looked at his Mom and Dad, then made his way over to Erney. Reaching out, Paul grabbed him by the collar and held him up close.

"I'm tired of your bull shit. You walk around here like you're a killer, but I've never heard of you being in a fight. In the future, when you talk to me, choose your words carefully. And say 'please.' I wouldn't want to show everyone that you're all bark and no bite."

Paul took a step backwards waiting for Erney's response, but the look on Erney's face told him there wouldn't be any. Erney got into his truck without saying a word. Paul mover his rig and let him out.

Paul called Alice and asked her to meet them at Spunky Steer Steakhouse. She was so happy, she was squealing over the phone. He told her to come as she was, to forget about cleaning up. He just wanted to see her.

Feeling like a true warrior, Paul wanted to show off his scars, so he asked his Mom to help him change his bandages. He removed his shirt, and she took off the old ones. First the arm. His Dad came over and inspected his arm. Mom disinfected the wounds, putting salve on them before re-dressing them. Next came his face. He had a mean cut on the right side; it would leave a nasty scar. Mom was delicate.

"Am I hurting you?"

Paul didn't say anything.

"You're going to have to have some plastic surgery done."

"No," Paul answered. "These are my battle scars. They are going to stay the way they are. Thanks for the help, Mom."

Upon arriving at the restaurant they put in their name and took seats waiting to be called. They weren't in a hurry; Alice wasn't there yet. Paul sat in between his parents.

"Ray spoke to me before I left. He sends his best to you and mom and hopes you will go back and see him real soon."

Alice came through the door and ran to Paul screaming when she saw his face. She made such a scene that everyone in the place had to come and see what was going on. As the other guests were ushered back to their seats, Alice clung to him around his neck and wouldn't let go.

"Are you all right? Your poor face. You'll have to have surgery."

"We'll talk about it later."

The waitress motioned them to follow her to a table. While they were enjoying their salads, Paul spoke up.

"You all know what I went up there for. Well, I accomplished what I set out to do, and now I'm healed. I haven't had a nightmare since this happened." He turned to Alice. "We can get married any time you want. I feel like I can take on the whole world."

"Yeah, but what actually happened?" Dad asked

"Not now. It'll make a good story next time we're out fishing."

"Since you've been gone, we've been busy. We knew our prayers would be answered, so I've been looking around and you know that little station down at the corner here. Well it's for sale. Six lots. I see a lot of potential here. We've got the money and we could make it work. It looks like you're on a winning streak, so if you're going into business, now's the time. Why don't we go down and look at it tomorrow."

"Okay," Paul didn't know what else to say. He was dumbstruck. Dad chuckled.

"There's something else."

"Gee, you have been busy."

"There's a house."

Alice looked at Paul.

"I think it's a nice house, close by. Good enough for a starter. If there's anything you don't like, we can change it. We drove by it with Alice, but she hasn't said anything yet."

"I'm waiting to see it with Paul. Then we can make up our minds."

The waitress brought diner and they ate mostly in silence. Under the table, Paul and Alice rubbed their feet against one another. They thought Mom and Dad didn't know what was going on, but Paul accidently mistook Dad's foot for Alice's. Dad looked at him, wondering if he was trying to signal to him. Paul looked back, puzzled. Then he realized what he had done, and that ended that. When they finished, Paul paid the bill. As they walked out the door, Dad and Paul were laughing. The two women couldn't figure out what was so funny until it dawned on Alice; she whispered it to Mom, and soon all four of them were doubled over.

In the morning Paul and his Dad drove down to the filling station. They parked across the street. The place was old, with antique pumps. It had two bays but no lifts. It did have a grease pit, but the lots were knee deep in grass. An old man, half asleep, sat in the office on a grungy sofa.

"You could clean it up, put up some signs, hire a kid to pump gas if you want. It'd be easy to add more bays. The lots go from the garage to those buildings down the street there."

"That's all part of this property?"

"Yup"

"What a waste."

"Maybe the old guy worked hard all his life."

Paul kicked a piece of gravel. "How much is he asking?"

"Oh, you know, too much."

"Well, that's how we work best."

They crossed the street and walked into the old man's office.

"Mind if we look around?"

"Help yourself," the man said, nodding off again.

They walked out into the bay area and made like they were sizing up the area. The old man got out of his chair and came to the door.

"What are you fellas looking for?"

"We're looking for a sale. You interested?"

"Maybe."

"Either you are or you aren't," Paul said, turning on his heels.

"Wait, no. I've been thinking about it."

"How much?"

"The buildings aren't much, but there are six lots that come with it."

Paul and Dad remained silent.

"Hundred thousand," the man said. "That's a fair price, considering."

They haggled a little, back and forth. Dad just looked out the window. The man started to get frustrated.

"By the look of you, I'm not sure this is even a conversation we need to be having. I mean, look at your face, son. You got any money in the first place, or am I wasting my time?"

"Come on, Paul," Dad said. "He doesn't want to sell. Those stalls out there are a hazard. The pumps have to be replaced. Lot's full of weeds. If I'm going to spend my money on a place for you, it's going to be better than this."

The old man got out of his chair. "How much you willing to pay, right now? Not tomorrow, but right now."

"Thirty-five, and that's it."

"Make it forty, and its yours."

"Well," Paul said, grinning. "I guess we bought me a shop."

Later, after they'd driven to the bank, Paul and Dad drove by the house Dad picked out for them.

"You don't have to tell Alice that we came by here if you don't want to. I know she wants to see it with you. But it's a good buy, and it would be a shame if some one else beat you to it."

"Is that the house?" Paul asked as they pulled up.

"That's it. The husband died about three months ago. His wife lives here alone, wants a quick sale. You see how nice the front is? The back is big, and just as nice. Three bedrooms and two baths. A little old, maybe, but in good shape. If you can get Alice to come down Saturday, we'll give it our one shot deal. Make an offer, take it or leave it. But I think they'll take it."

"Sounds good," Paul said, and they headed back home.

Anxious about the house, Alice arrived early on Saturday morning. After breakfast they all went down there. Dad and Mom walked around outside. Dad had been there earlier, and the woman was happy newlyweds were buying the house. She was packing small things in preparation to move.

"When are you planning to move?"

"We haven't made you an offer yet," Paul said.

"Oh, your dad and I already took care of that. We already contacted our mover and will be out in two days. You can move right in."

They thanked her and went out back with Mom and Dad.

"I bought a house, and I don't even know what I paid for it," Paul said to Dad.

"Don't worry, I got you a good deal. Too good. So what do you think of your new place?"

Paul gave him a big hug. Alice was hugging Mom with tears in her eyes.

"There was a time when I thought I would never get Paul to marry me, but when he makes up his mind, things go so fast it makes my head spin. I hope it never stops."

After the old lady moved out, they went through the house, ridding themselves of the old furniture and replacing it with new things Alice and Mom had picked out. Paul had started to tidy up the station. He surveyed it, deciding what would stay and what would go, which things needed to be replaced, and what would do for now. A teenager strolled into the lot off the street.

"My name is Jimmy. Are you the new owner here?"

Paul hadn't been expecting company.

"Sure .Why do you ask?"

"You need me."

"What makes you say that?"

"Because I'm a hard worker, and I'm honest. I'll work for you pretty cheap. Just let me show you what I can do."

Paul certainly needed the help, he couldn't deny that. And this boy looked to be all right.

"When can you start?"

"Now, if you want."

Where did this guy come from, Paul wondered. How did hired help fall into my lap? He knew one thing for sure: he wasn't going to question his fortune.

"You can start by hauling those boxes in the back out to the dumpster. I'll have more for you when you get back."

Jimmy was gone only a few minutes when he called Paul to come out back. As Paul approached, Jimmy opened one of the boxes. Paul looked in. It wasn't junk. It was cans of paint, with trays and brushes, even office supplies.

"New plan. Bring all the paint supplies inside, and the rest put in my office." Maybe he had a winner here with Jimmy, Paul thought. With his help, Paul spent the rest the day and the day after cleaning and preparing the place for paint.

Paul And Alice went to the church and made arrangements for their wedding. They could get married right away, on the same date as Alice's parents' wedding. It only gave them two weeks to plan, so they called to invite people rather than sending formal invitations, which would take two weeks just for people to receive them. Instead, invitations were made over the phone.

The wedding was beautiful, and the reception was at the new house. The gifts were all put in one bedroom. Everything was just so, the food, the drinks, the decorations. They pushed what little furniture they had against the walls to make room for dancing. Alice glowed.

Paul chatted with Bill Morgan in the kitchen.

"It's about time you got married, Paul. Now you and I can take the kids and go fishing."

"We have to have kids, first," Alice said, creeping up behind them. Paul laughed, kissing Alice on the forehead.

The newlyweds went upstairs to change before dancing to the anniversary waltz. Then everyone took over the floor, and the room writhed with merriment. Erney, who had a few drinks, congratulated Paul and hung one on Alice. She just laughed it off and looked at his wife. Erney turned to Paul.

"I need to talk to you about what you said at Dad's the other day."

Great, Paul thought, there goes my wedding day. It was going so well, too.

The brothers walked out the back door. Erney rolled up his sleeves and stopped.

"I've been thinking about what you said."

"And?"

"And you're right, I've been out of line lately. So since it's your wedding day and all, I just wanted to say I'm sorry. I know we'll always be brothers, but I want us to be friends, too."

Paul said nothing, just stood there in silence. Erney knit his eyebrows, unsure of what would happen next. Then Paul's arms were suddenly wrapped around his brother.

As they embraced, cheers erupted from the house. They both turned to see the entire wedding party peeking out the windows.

"You certainly found a way to steal the show," Paul said.

Alice ran out and threw his arms around him. She kissed him until he could barely breathe. Maybe it was still his day, after all.

Paul and Alice celebrated their honeymoon in their new home.

"I got a call from my boss. He wanted to congratulate us," Alice said as they sifted through all the gifts. "He said he left a card for us, and that I should call him once I open it."

"Wonder what that's all about."

The pair rifled through cards until they found the right one. Alice opened it, accidentally letting the check inside flutter out of the envelope and onto her lap. She gasped when she read the letter.

"What is it? Don't just gasp like that, tell me!"

"He says he's buying a new store in Riverside, and he wants me to help manage. Paul, this is perfect. I could be close to home." Alice clapped her hands together. "Should I do it?"

"Seems like you should, based on your reaction. Sweetie, whatever you want to do is fine by me."

The bad thing about having there reception at the house was that they had to clean up the mess. The day after, Paul was putting the trash in his barrels and planed to haul some down to dumpsters at the station. As Paul was picking up the decoration boxes and putting them in the garage, Jimmy walked in with two of his buddies.

"Where do we start?"

"What?"

"I know you got hitched yesterday. Figured you'd need a clean-up crew."

Paul felt this was suspicious. He had learned not to trust anyone who was too generous with their time and energy.

"Ok, the jig's up. Why the hell are you being so nice? You've got no reason and no incentive. Give it to me straight, kid."

Jimmy hung his head.

"I remember when you used to do tune-ups before you disappeared. You're self-taught, and you're the best. I just want to be like you."

Paul felt his face flush, quickly patting Jimmy on the back.

Alice came by later to see how things were going and to bring Paul some lunch. The place was already spic and span.

"Boy when you do something, you do it big. Where did you find them? I didn't know there were any hard-working young men left in this town. I thought I married the last one."

"Jimmy," Paul said, "This is Alice. My wife, as of yesterday. Alice, this is Jimmy. My assistant, as of the day before that."

Valmore Valiquette

"Pleasure to meet you, Jimmy. Paul, I have some wedding cake left and coffee to go with it. Why don't you sit down for a minute and enjoy it, before it goes bad."

CHAPTER THIRTEEN

Meanwhile, up North, Ray asked Jim over for a talk. They sat around the table drinking coffee.

"I speak for all of us," Ray said. "And the suspense is killing us. We know Paul came up here in his fancy boat. Joseph was about to turn him away. Of course, we were surprised to see him here after what he'd done and wondered what he wanted. When he said he wanted a canoe to go up back country, we thought he was insane or suicidal. I let him take my canoe, and the next time we saw him he was with you. He looked pretty badly messed up, but he had a look of satisfaction I can't quite place. He told Joseph he had a problem of some kind and the only way he could solve it was to go up there alone. So would you please tell us what happened, Jim?"

"Paul made me promise not to tell. He told me not to tell anyone what was wrong or what happened." He didn't want to break his promise, but Jim felt a stronger obligation towards his father than Paul. "That evening when I arrived, Mary told us what happened here and was afraid for him. The way he handled your canoe scared her I guess. I thought I taught him better, but then he was alone and according to what she said, his load was off balance.

"You know I always liked Paul, so I figured I would go and help him do whatever he had to do. Even though he was with us for a while he still thought like a sportsman. Somehow he made it to the place where we killed and dressed or the first moose. Must've made it there in daylight because he'd had enough time to make a perch in the trees to sleep on. By the time I got there it was dark already, and three wolves were attacking him. He shot two of them with a shotgun while they were still on him, then the third one started pulling at his arm. I shot, and I think I hit him, but Paul killed him with the knife.

"When I got to him, he pulled himself out of what was left of his sleeping bag. I asked him if he didn't have a mental problem, what with him coming all this way to make himself wolf bait. Then he told me what happened to him. I told you how we saw a beaver up close when I was stalking that moose. I knew something happened to him, but when he didn't say anything I let it go. When we were attacked at the falls he acted kind of strange, but I just assumed it was how Americans acted in those kinds of situations. It all just kept building and building, all the weird ways he was acting, until the catastrophe with Mr. Jacques. He told me in the woods that he'd been trying to control his fear as best he could, but after Mr. Jacques was killed, he cracked. Had nightmares every night except when he took some pills a doctor gave him, which he stopped taking. He came back to confront his nightmares, get his fear back in his grasp.

"Aside from not knowing what he was doing, he did something no one here would have dared to do. They said he was a coward, but he has more guts than anyone. Yes, what he did was stupid, but he figured he had to do it, and he licked his problem. When he left here all cut up he was a changed man. I know he'll stay down there where he comes from, and I'll probably never see him again, but I'm glad I got to know him for a short while at least."

Jim looked to Mary. She hadn't made a sound the whole time he was telling his story. Her face was red and wet. She made her way to her bedroom, flopped on the bed and let it all out.

"Oh, my poor Paul. How I misjudged you, and now you're gone."

CHAPTER FOURTEEN

The day after the wedding, Paul got a phone call from one of his old buddies when he came home from work. Paul told him he got married, and he congratulated him.

"Your father told me what you've been up to. I hope you haven't forgotten me. I don't care if work is slow for a while or if we do some specials and work for a little less. I'd just do a little more work. I'd even move to be closer to the shop if you wanted."

"I'm going to run my shop a little different than we're used to. First of all, no comebacks or complaints. The customer in my shop will always be right even if we don't make money. Of course I won't be put upon by some wise guy either. I'm going to have a bunch of different shops here so they can all lean on each other and push business in each other's directions. There are six lots here and I plan to fill them with different auto trades. I know you're a good tune-up specialist and would fit in perfectly. I'll call you when I'm ready for you."

"Boy am I glad I followed up on your promise. Thanks, Paul."

Paul kept his promise and worked out his plans. He took out the pumps but left the tanks, which were in pretty good shape.

He re-did the front of the garage to make it a shop instead of a filling station, got his friend Mike to work as a partner.

When Paul wasn't there, Jimmy worked for Mike; however, he soon surpassed him in skill, and people started asking for Jimmy by name instead of Mike. Mike didn't mind because he made the money. One day Jimmy went to visit Paul.

"I don't mean to brag, but I think I'm ready for my own shop. I'm not going to quit because you been a good friend. But if you want to start another shop keep me in mind. Also, I've been teaching a friend of mine on the side, and he's getting pretty good at tune-ups and engine repairs. He's doing like you did, working in his fathers garage. So keep us in mind, okay?"

Instead of shaking hands, they hugged.

"What ever you do, Jimmy, I want you to keep in touch with me," Paul said. "Remember what you said when you first came up to me at the station. I need you, and I won't forget that."

Soon an architect came in to help Paul figure out how to get as much as he could from all the lots he now owned, thinking of putting in shops and other retail businesses. It was a little hectic with all the construction going on. He made contact with tradespeople so that when the construction was finished, they would be ready to move in. Naturally, there would be a big celebration.

One of the shops was of an odd shape, though, and Paul had a hard time finding someone to put a business in there. He called Jimmy and said he wanted a visit. That evening Jimmy and his wife came by for dinner. Afterwards, Paul poured drinks and they sat in the living room.

"I have a problem, Jimmy, and I need your help."

"You know I'm here for you. What's up?"

"See, I've got the lots all divided into shops, but one's got kind of a funny shape to it. I'm thinking of putting in a boat repair facility."

"Boat repairs?"

"You would have to learn the particulars, but there's no competition. I know we're a ways from water, but they pull boats around and if you develop a reputation it would be a good place to get a jumpstart in that business. Oh, and I would back you for a percentage. In other words, I wouldn't let you fail. Think it over and let me know.

"We've been together for quite some time now and we get along just fine in everything we do. Why don't we go ahead with this and make it work? I can probably get some of my friends involved. Maybe I can even get someone I know to go work at a boat shop for some experience."

Paul liked the idea, and it was agreed.

So all the shops were working bringing in rent. Paul only had to go around once in a while to see that they were being kept clean. He set up a meeting once a month with free beer so each shop owner could say how he was doing, and if needed, how Paul could help them.

In the five years that had passed since their marriage, Paul had work done on his house to make Alice happy. After the remodeling was done, he had a party so he could show off his craftsmanship. Dad and Mom were there; Jimmy, Mike and Erney all came with their wives. There was a buffet with lots of beer. The girls stayed in the house talking women's stuff; the men were out in the back drinking beer and trying to cheat at horseshoes. Everyone had a great time.

Everything was going as Paul and his father had planed. Even though she didn't have to work anymore, Alice was happy to stay on at her job. Paul had good people working with him and for him; Dad was at a loss, he didn't have anything to do. When he complained, Paul would tell him to go fishing.

Paul missed his time out to go fishing. Mike had a rubber boat that was easy to carry. One day Paul wanted to go fishing, but not alone. So he asked Alice if she would go with him. They loaded his truck and went out to a small lake Jimmy had told him about that didn't allow outboard motors. When they got there they loaded some of there fishing gear, food for snacks and bait in the boat. Paul brought two paddles, even though he knew he would do most of the paddling.

They had made their way almost around the lake, having had only nibbles but no real bites, when everything started trembling like there was an earthquake. The water had tiny ripples jumping up on the surface. There was a gush, and a whirlpool appeared, sucking down water like a drain. Paul didn't like what he saw and called to Alice to paddle real hard with him so they could make it to shore. They were really digging in to the water but to no avail. They were being sucked into the hole.

"No matter what happens, hang onto the boat and don't let go."

The boat started slipping into the sinkhole, taking Alice with it.

"I love you, Paul," she said, and she disappeared beneath the water.

Paul hung onto the boat and it came to a halt as the whirlpool ceased. The water rushed in around him. He let go of the boat and swam to the surface, which was only about ten feet up. When he surfaced he noticed that the hole was full of water and the lake had calmed down. There were people on the shore, hollering encouragements to him. No one came to help.

There was a small fishing shack a hundred yards away. He made his way there, but there was no phone. He was told that someone had gone to an outside phone and was calling for help. Someone would be coming soon. Paul walked back to the side of the lake where he lost Alice and looked at where she went down, wondering if he would ever see her again.

A police car drove up, followed by an ambulance and a fire truck. Paul wondered what they could even do.

"What happened here?"

"My wife and I were fishing when an earthquake or something occurred and our boat was sucked under the water like it was going down a sewer."

"How did you get out?"

"I held onto the boat, and it must have plugged the hole that the water was going down into. She must be on the other side of the boat. What are you going to do to get her out of there?"

"Not much we can do. At least not until better equipment arrives."

When the scuba team made it to the lake, they had a similar response. It didn't seem like much could be done at all. All the emergency vehicles were leaving. Paul motioned to one of the scuba divers and took him aside.

"We can go down there and get her. I need your help,"

"I'm sorry, we can't. Too much water, it's too dangerous."

"And without the water?"

Paul ran back to the fishing shack and called Jimmy. In no time, Paul had a rowboat, a two by four, some long nails and plenty of rope. Paul hammered a couple nails into the end of the two by four. The board and rope were put into the boat. Putting on borrowed scuba equipment, Paul and the diver descended into the hole. Paul directed him to where the boat was stuck, and they wedged the board into the side of the opening between the boat and the hole. Then they tied the rope to the board so that when the rope was pulled it would puncture the rubber boat, letting the air out. Hopefully this would allow the water to continue flowing through the hole that the boat had plugged. They returned to the surface, got in the boat and together pulled on the rope. Immediately the water started down the big hole again until the cavern at the bottom of the hole could be seen. They maneuvered the boat so the rear end was over the hole, then tied off the ropes so they could lower themselves down into the cavern. Once inside they noticed that the rubber boat was gone, and in its place was a large hole big enough to crawl through.

Paul took the lead and went through the opening. They went about ten feet into the hole, where it kind of opened up.

There, hanging from a rock outcropping, was Alice. Her lifejacket strap was caught on the rock. Evidently she was sucked through the hole and as she went by the rock her life jacket got hooked up, stopping her from going further down the hole. Paul went to her, taking her around the waist and easing her back out of the hole.

At the funeral, a Mass was said for Alice, and all her friends were there. Again the reception was set up at the house. It was a good way to say goodbye to her.

Over and over Paul had to explain what had happened. He'd learned that when the oil companies sucked the oil out from underground, it left a huge hole that remained because of the rock-lined cavern. When the earthquake happened, the water pressure over the cavern forced the roof of the cave to give way and allowed the water to submerge into the cavern and flow out the way the oil did.

"We just happened to be in the wrong place at the wrong time," he found himself saying over and over.

Paul would always remember her. But he would rent the house; he didn't want to live in it without her.

As time passed, Paul's business prospered without much effort on his part; Mark and his wife had everything under control. They did such a good job at managing property that other property owners hired their business to run their property for them. They were busy and they liked it, so Paul left them alone unless there was something important that took his opinion to solve. His garage rent worked well. Like Dad said, it was a good investment.

Jimmy's boat business needed expansion and Mark was looking for a bigger place closer to the ocean so he could handle larger boats. He was also handling insurance claims and wanted to have room to do canvas repairs and installation. Paul admired the way Jimmy was always looking for ways to expand his operation.

But Paul couldn't live in the house anymore, and he didn't like the idea of living alone again, so he moved back in with his parents. In exchange for letting him stay (even though they never asked for anything in return in the first place), Paul renovated the house and added extensions so they would all be more comfortable. He had even given Mom better appliances for her kitchen. Paul's room was modernized as well, now more spacious and fitted out with new furniture.

He was very comfortable in his new bed. He started dreaming about Alice. She would come and go as if she were a specter; all he wanted to reach out and touch her. She put her hand on his chest.

"Don't worry about me. Where I am now is beautiful, and I am at peace. Maybe somewhere in time we will be together again, but for now, I want you to go on living your life and be happy."

Then she was disappearing again, blowing him a kiss.

He awoke with a start and looked up at the ceiling, Could it be that she came to him and was never to come back to him again? Was that her farewell?

He went back to sleep and awoke in the morning with the sun shining through the window. He lay there for a while, thinking about his dream.

At breakfast he mentioned his dream to his parents.

"She was a good girl and is in heaven at peace," Mom said. "So listen to her and stop worrying."

Living with his parents, Paul was able to watch over them. He spent more time with his Dad playing cards and cribbage. Mom, who liked to knit once in a while, did more of it now so she could be in the living room with both her son and her husband. They talked about all kinds of things. Paul sensed that his parents were slowly getting their affairs in order, so when the time came most things would be taken care of. His Dad walked with a cane now and lost his breath when he walked to far.

One afternoon Paul and Dad were talking in the backyard.

"I would like to have all the children over for a gathering, barbeque or something so I can talk to you all. Can you set this up for me?"

"Sure, I'll take care of it right away."

It was set for that weekend: a barbeque in the backyard with beer and horseshoes again. When dinner was over, Dad sat at one of the tables and said loud enough for everyone to hear that he wanted them to stop what they were doing and gather around, that he had something to say. He cleared his throat.

"I may not be with you for very much longer, so I want your undivided attention. I don't want any interruptions. I want you to know of my decisions before I leave. I definitely don't want any squabbling. As you all know Paul and I have a little business between us that we've been working for a long time. Our agreement is that the survivor takes all. The business gave your mother and I an Income and a good life. When I pass it all goes to Paul. I have a small bank account and some small investments and personal things, but it all goes to your mother for her to do with it what she pleases.

"I know we have had problems in the past, but my dying wish is that you all put your problems aside and develop better relations between yourselves. I love you all and will pass knowing that you all love and forgive me for anything I may have done to offend you. I don't want you to cry over me. My life with your mother has been beyond expectations. I don't know how I can go to a better place. If you have any questions you can work them out with your Mother and Paul. They have my power of attorney and are handling my will. Thank you all for coming. Enjoy your day and pray for me."

With that he closed his eyes to rest. Paul wheeled him back into the house and put him to bed. The exertion tired him out. He had terminal cancer, which was slowly eating away at him.

He lost all ambition and wanted to stay in the house all the time watching TV. He knew it was coming and wasn't going to fight it. Mom was taking it very well in Paul's estimation, keeping all her emotions inside. Paul watched and talked to her about happy things so she wouldn't have a nervous breakdown.

After their guests left, Paul went out to his boat and removed the cover. It still looked good Paul periodically went over it to keep it in top shape. Being next to the boat made him relax.

He thought about his life, how Dad had helped him. Dad was the one who started him out repairing cars, had convinced him to save his money and invest in rentals. Then there had been the trip North; the outcome was traumatic, and Dad had been there to comfort him. And then the lake, and Alice. Dad had been there for that, too. Paul had put him—and Mom—through hell, and they never complained. In fact, just the opposite, they had insisted on helping. Now Dad was leaving and he would be alone with Mom.

He felt some one near him, at his elbow. He turned, and there was Mom.

"I know what you're going through with your father, but remember we still have each other to take care of." They looked into each other's eyes in silent conversation and suddenly they hugged, and the tears flowed.

Mom helped him put the cover back on his boat, and they went back into the house. Mom had already taken care of Dad's dinner and had something for Paul to eat.

Paul wondered what was going to happen now. He wondered where Mary was. Had she ever married, had children? Was she happy? He was convinced that if he'd stayed with her and brought her down to California, she would have been in the movies, become a model or something. As Paul was eating he mentioned that he was wondering what happened to her.

"It's funny you mention that. You father wrote to his brother Joe to find out how he was doing. He wrote back just today that

Valmore Valiquette

he was fine but had a hard time getting around, so his trips were over.

"He sent his condolences to you on losing your wife, and that it seems like you've been pretty unlucky with women. Mary never married. Ray died a little after you left there, Ray's wife Mofet moved back to Barrens Landing, which is where her people were on the reservation. The boys followed her; Jim is still fishing the lake and runs a trap line in the winter, hasn't seen a wolf since you left. They say you got them all, but know it only takes a few years for them to bring up their numbers. The fishery was dismantled and moved to another location. The school had closed, so people were leaving. Joe said the Jacques family was the last to go, that they tried to sell but had no takers."

Paul stayed around the house a much as possible. Dad spent a lot of time in bed, and his doctor said he didn't have much longer. Mom walked around in a daze. She was forgetful and had to be careful not to burn herself at the stove. She would walk to church so she could pray for Dad's recovery and forgiveness. The priest told her that God had a field of flowers and once in a while he would pick a few. People went to him by invitation only, he had told her, so she should pray and keep herself in the state of grace. He would come now and again to visit Dad, forgiving him his sins and giving him his last rights.

One morning, seemingly like any other, Paul awoke and went into the kitchen where Mom was preparing his breakfast. These days she would make up a tray and bring it in to Dad so he would have something to eat. When she went in that morning she thought he was asleep and put the tray on the dresser and tried to wake him. She called Paul to come and help her.

When Paul came in he examined his father and took his pulse. There was none. He took the tray and asked Mom to follow him back into the kitchen. He sat with her at the table and looked at her. She knew. She had expected it to happen, but now Paul imagined she would be lost without him

The Innocent Beaver of Big Black River

"I've been expecting it to happen at any time, he was failing so bad," she said. She was strong and looked like she would be all right after the first shock had passed.

"I'll make all the preparations and calls. I'll ask Rose and Erney to come over and stay with us so we can all be together. Will that be all right?"

"If they want to come, I would appreciate the help."

Paul called Dad's doctor who said he would take care of all the proper documents. Erney's wife, Rose, arrived and stayed with Mom. Paul made phone calls to the relatives. Uncle Joe said he would come. Paul said he could stay with him and Mom.

The funeral parlor had a nice service for Dad. Paul thought they made him look good. A Mass was said before Dad was put in his crypt, where he would rest in peace. Paul had a catered affair at home; he didn't want Mom to have to cook or clean. Eventually everyone talked themselves out and went home. Erney and his wife decided to stay over; Uncle Joe stayed with his brother Henry.

After Erney and his wife left the next morning, Uncle Joe came back to stay with Paul and Mom. Paul and Uncle Joe sat in the living room, talking about Dad and Big Black River. Uncle Joe brought up Mary, mentioned again how she'd never married. She moved to Winnipeg and got a job there. It wasn't far off from what Mom had told him: she dated but never found anyone she liked enough to marry, and Ray died shortly after Paul had left. Jim built a cabin at the reservation but spent the winters at his daughter's in Winnipeg. It was all old news, but Paul listened, anyway.

"You know you're still welcome up there," Joe said. "They would have invited you but figured you wouldn't want to go back."

Joe spent a few more days with them, and Paul and Mom were happy for the company. But even at his age, Joe still got wanderlust and said he had to move on. He said he would go to Hawaii but at the last minute he went back to Boston. The day he planned to leave there was a knock on the door. Mom was greeted by a gentleman claiming to be a friend of Dad's; he said was coming by to give his condolences.

"I'm sorry, but how do you know our family?"

"I'm an old friend of your husband's," he said. "And I'm also Paul's doctor."

Mom called Paul to the door where he said hello to the doctor.

"I was hoping to schedule a little follow-up exam."

"Thanks, but I think I'm doing just fine now." Paul remembered how the doctor strung him up and really didn't do him much good. "What is it really? There some debt we haven't paid?"

"Oh, no, just the opposite." The doctor straightened his glasses on his nose. "Your father helped me start my practice; I'm the one with the debt to pay. Treating you was part of my repaying him, and since he passed I've been looking over the journals I made of our conversations. I thought you might be interested in hearing my analysis of our sessions. And of course, there'll be no charge."

With his eyes, Joe indicated to Paul that this was an offer he should accept. What did he have to lose?

The appointment was on a Monday morning at ten o'clock. When he walked into the waiting room, there was no receptionist. Instead, the doctor received him with a handshake and took him into his office.

"How's it going, Paul? The last time you were here, I think things were a little confusing for both of us: you didn't think I was doing you much good, and I thought you were going to take your anger out on me after you left and came back. Then of all things you thanked me, and I never heard from you again." The doctor sat down and gestured to Paul to do the same. "I want to tell you that I never stopped working on your case, and I think I've finally come up with some sort of conclusion. But first I want to hear what you did with my advice. What'd you do to get rid of your fear? Start with what you did when you left here and don't leave out any details

Suddenly Paul wondered what had possessed him to come back here. What could this possibly accomplish? But he felt compelled to oblige the doctor.

"I took my equipment and traveled back to the river. I borrowed a canoe and traveled up the river to where we had shot a moose. I made camp and waited for them to come at me. I shot two of them and killed the third with my knife. After it was all over I felt good, like I could take on the whole world. I didn't know it but my cousin Jim followed me there to help me. I told him of my nightmares, and he said he didn't know how killing wolves would cure nightmares. We traveled down the river in the dark, and I followed him back to the landing. At the camp he stopped the bleeding a little and at the landing insisted on bandaging me up the rest of the way before I left to make my journey back. Mary helped. I had food in the boat so I declined their offer to stay for a meal; I just wanted to get out of there. I went there to accomplish something and I did it, so it was time to go home.

After I got back I decided to settle down with my girlfriend, Alice. We got married, and for a while things were perfect. I had a beautiful wife and a booming business. My luck continued until I lost my wife and now my Dad. I don't know what's next, but after all that I think I'm ready for whatever comes my way."

The Doctor studied Paul's face for a minute. Paul felt exposed, vulnerable; had he said too much? Had he said the wrong thing? Was the doctor going to say he was still crazy?

"Your problem wasn't with the wolves," the doctor said. Paul felt the color drain from his face. "You haven't been listening. I went to a seminar where I got to talk to some other doctors about the problem of patients with unresolved issues; I told them about your wolf crisis. They talked it over for a day and came to the conclusion that it was the girl."

Paul looked surprise but wanted to hear more. The doctor continued.

"You went up there a typical bachelor with a girlfriend pressuring you to marry her. You were glad to get away for a while; anyone in your position would be. No doubt you really enjoyed your cousins. When you met Mary, you saw something exotic and new; likely Mary saw her chance to leave Winnipeg and see the world. Not to say you weren't really in love. Of course you were. After the two of you decided to get married, you must have made a lot of music. Maybe you even forgot how afraid you were to commit and settle down. But when Mrs. Jacques started at you with her rage, you cracked.

"As for your dreams about the wolves, you blame them for your break-up with Mary. You believe you lost her because of the wolves. You can't dream of her so you dream of the wolves. By killing the wolves, in your mind you severed any relationship or love you had for her. When you were at Jim's house being bandaged up you could have rekindled your love for her. She was giving you that chance. You would have been a hero again as soon as they found out what you did in the woods. But you didn't figure it that way. You rejected her. You couldn't get out of there fast enough. Maybe you solved your problem with fear, Paul, but you still have your problem with Mary. And it could be that you never think about Mary again, but remember that she was important enough to you to make you lose your mind."

Paul leaned back in his chair and breathed deeply. Had it really been Mary and not the wolves all this time? He leaned forward again, resting his elbows on his knees.

"I *have* had thoughts about Mary, now that you mention it. She's never really left my mind."

"You know, Paul, I bet she regrets what she did."

"How do you figure?"

"I don't think she would've broken off the engagement if Mrs. Jacques hadn't been so hysterical. Situations like that make people cause people to have drastic reactions. You of all people should know that."

Paul thanked the Doctor and made an offer to pay, but the doctor refused to accept, reminding Paul that he was the one indebted

"Keep in touch, Paul, ok? I feel like we're friends now."

Paul shook the doctor's hand as a sort of gentleman's agreement. On his way home he thought a lot about what they discussed. He was ashamed of his having feelings for Mary so soon after Alice's passing, but nevertheless he couldn't stop himself from dreaming about what the future might hold.

CHAPTER FIFTEEN

As he entered the house he noticed Mom had lunch ready.

"What did the doctor have to say that was so important?" She didn't usually get involved. She used to let Dad handle Paul's problems.

Paul told her of the doctor's opinion as to what caused Paul's problem.

"Do you still love her?"

"I don't know. She's always been in the back of my mind, but I figured it was because I did love her. But I went through a lot with her."

"Well, what *are* you going to do now? You being alone and all."

"I don't know. I guess I'll take it one day at a time and do the best I can."

They finished lunch and Paul made a few phone calls pertaining to his business. He was contemplating buying more rental property for Mark to manage. He had a building he wanted to buy, but the owners wanted too much for it. They wanted to rent it to him so he could rent it to someone else. It didn't make much sense to Paul, so he called Mark.

"I took care of it," Mark said.

"You did?"

"The thing with Mr. Rizor? Yeah, it's all done. You must've spoken to the wrong person because his son sold it to us for our price. It'll take a while for escrow to close, but it's in the bag."

"You always amaze me," Paul said with a chuckle. "In fact, you amaze me so much I think I'll go fishing and let you run things."

"Now that's a good Idea. I'll tell Jean to take this one over when it comes, that you have something for me to do for you and we'll take off for June Lake. Of course, I'll have to mention that you didn't tell me what you wanted."

Mark replaced the small boat lost in the lake accident. It was a small Bayliner with an 85 horsepower motor. It was a gift from the company they bought the river cruisers from. Mark enlisted Jimmy's help with the purchase of the river cruisers and got them to throw in the Bayliner, trailer and motors.

As Paul and Mark traveled along they talked about the business.

"I'm happy the way our business relations have worked out. You're doing a very good job for me. When I leave I don't have to worry, because I know my business is in good hands."

"To tell you the truth, the best decision we made was to put Jean on as a manager. With her experience from the insurance company she can really handle people and unpleasant situations. Honestly I don't know what I'd do without her around."

They found a good camping spot and started fishing right away. They kept some nice ones and threw the rest back. That evening they sat around drinking beer and eating fish until they felt overstuffed.

"I want you to know that if things continue working out the way they are, there's a large promotion in the works for you," Paul said. "I'm thinking of a partnership. What do you think? Would you and Jean like to be partners in my business ventures?"

Mark sat speechless for a while.

"Me and Jean have worked hard trying to make the right decisions for you. I know you're a fair person, but a partnership? Are you sure you want to do this? You could be a millionaire if you kept if for yourself. Why share with us?"

"Because you deserve it, simple as that. So it's settled, then. When we get back we'll draw up papers and make it legal."

The two men came home three days later, and the next day Mark invited Paul to his house for dinner. Paul arrived around six o'clock, and they sat in the living room. Jean wanted to them to sit down to eat, but Mark stopped her.

"We have something more important to tell you."

"What could be more important than sitting down and eat a hot meal?"

"A partnership in Paul's business."

"You've got to be kidding." Jean slapped her hand over her mouth. Mark stood up.

"He told me while we were up fishing, what do you think?" Mark asked. Jean went to Paul put her arms around his neck and gave him a big hug.

"Yes, yes, yes!" Jean held Paul at arms length and smiled at him. Then she skipped back over to her husband, giggling. "And now that we're partners, I've got some news I've been holding back. I'm pregnant."

Mark grabbed her and kissed her. Paul was all smiles, happy for both of them.

"We'll keep going as usual, of course. This won't change things," Paul said as they sat down to dinner. "We'll have meetings once a month, everyone gets their own salary."

"Are you sure?" Mark asked.

"Now that your family is growing, you'll need it."

At breakfast the next morning, Mom said she was thinking of going to live with Erney and June. After Paul told her that he made Mark a partner in his business, she thought he would be gone a lot more; she couldn't stand being alone in the house. Erney and June started visiting more. Sometimes they would bring the children; they wanted them to get to know their grandmother since she would be living with them now, and Mom was happy to have grandkids to pamper and adore. She would take some of her furniture and leave the rest for Paul. He knew he could rent the house, but he decided he would live in it and keep it in case she wanted to move back in someday.

Paul went about his business. Mark and Jean took hold of the reins and steered a good path. Under their management, the business prospered. They doubled their income in no time and had enough money to hire an accountant out of college. Paul taught all his new employees to treat the business as a family; bickering and gossiping would under no circumstances be tolerated.

Uncle Joe wrote asking how thing were. He wanted to take another trip, possibly to New Zealand and Australia, but he worried it would be too much for him. He wasn't getting any younger. He decided to come and visit for a week if it was all right with them. Mom sent him a welcome letter but asked that he bring his wife, Bertha; she also insisted they stay two weeks.

In a week they arrived. Bertha visited with Mom and Joe visited with Paul and sometimes with Erney. They would sit and talk, mostly about how proud Dad was of Paul's accomplishments. Paul explained that he couldn't have done what he did without Dad's help.

On the fourth day of Joe's visit, the mailman delivered a letter from Mary to Paul. Paul went into his bedroom and read his letter.

> Dear Paul,
>
> How are you? I received a letter from Uncle Joe. He told me you're alone now. I want to send my condolences for the death of your wife and father. I know the rest of my family wishes you

the same peace of mind and spirit that I do. Our father passed away as well, and we know what you're going through. We miss him and know you must miss your dad very much. My father spoke highly of him, and it was too bad that they didn't spend more time together.

The story of your wife's passing was unbelievable. Even though I never met her, I'm sorry for your loss. She must have been a wonderful person. How come you never had children?

I know we've had a rocky past, but nonetheless it would be nice to see you again. Come if you can. We have a lot to talk about.

I still love you.

Mary

Paul sat there on the bed, thinking about her letter. He would have to send her a response, but what would he say? Maybe—just maybe—their destiny would bring them back together again, but would they achieve the same feeling that they had for each other?

He went into the kitchen where Joe and Bertha and Mom were speaking in French. They were talking about their youth, how Dad and Mom had it tough, having one child after another.

"We loved every one of them and would do it all over again, God willing. How are your two children doing? Do you have many grandchildren?"

"We have enough to keep us busy."

Joe turned when he saw Paul was back.

"What did she write?"

"Uncle Joe, I don't want to be disrespectful, but it's kind of personal. She sends her and her family's condolences."

"Are you going to write back to her?"

"I think so."

"Good. She has been punishing herself too long for losing you. Everyone around her has been trying to convince her to date others but she refuses to. She considered the nunnery according to her parents but figured her love for you would interfere with her love for God."

Paul nodded and went back to his work. He had nothing to say.

When he had finished up with the paperwork and phone calls he had to make, he rejoined the conversation. To his relief, the subject had changed. Joe was saying that Mom and Paul should visit him and Bertha in Boston. Paul knew this was almost impossible. Mom couldn't travel alone, and he was up to his ears in his business. But he didn't want to seem ungrateful for the offer, so he didn't say anything about it.

Joe and Bertha stayed a few more days and made his plans to leave. Paul and Mom saw him and Bertha of to the airport. They hugged and kissed and wished each other good health and happiness. They were getting old; Paul wondered if he would ever see them again.

On the way home, Paul and Mom stopped by the office, where Paul was told there was some rental property for sale. Jean had been managing it for a customer, and when he wanted to sell it, he came to her first. Paul was proud of Jean's work; with her help, his business was now well known. It seemed all of his employees were prospering: Mark had taken on a construction company and Jimmy's boat shop was blossoming. As Paul drove home he surveyed his success in his mind; with the way his business was going, he could relax and let everything run itself.

But Paul was still alone. He cooked meals for one and watched TV as he ate them. Late that night, feeling sick of television and loneliness, he went into the study and started writing a letter to Mary.

Valmore Valiquette

Dear Mary

I must say I was surprised to receive your letter. But it was a welcome surprise. In the last five years I've thought about you a lot, wondering how you were and what you were doing. I talked to Uncle Joe and he filled me in on everything going on up there in Winnipeg.

Yes, I've been going through a very tough time, first losing my wife then my dad. My mom might move in with my brother and his wife because she feels that I have a life of my own to live and doesn't want to stand in my way. Other things are good, though. My business runs itself, and I have great friends working for me. But I have no love life.

I'm glad you wrote to me. Maybe we can pick up where we left off before I had my problem. When I feel lonely I sometimes remember us together out on the point holding one another, wanting one another. If you had your way we would have done it right there in the snow, with Jim and Jean watching us from their kitchen window. It was a good thing the wolves were running around or God knows what would have happened.

My doctor tells me now that the problem I thought was wolves was really you. That day in the snowmobile made us all act in ways we shouldn't have, and I had held on to hope that maybe you didn't mean what you said to me after the attack.

Anyway, this is all in the past. If you feel like I do, maybe we can pick up where we left off. Write me back soon.

Love you always,

Paul

CHAPTER SIXTEEN

Plans had been made for an ocean fishing trip with Mark and Jimmy. Jimmy acquired a good-sized cabin cruiser—purchased by the company—and this was supposed to be its maiden voyage. Some of Jimmy's employees served as the crew. Later a permanent crew would be found, and the boat would be put up for rent.

They went out early and used the fish finder made a good catch of tuna.

"We did good," Jimmy said. "The first time out we had a good catch. Nice way of christening our fishing boat, huh? Anyone bring any Champagne?"

They all laughed. Paul was happy knowing that his group got along well together. Having pulled in such a large catch, they decided to head for shore early. On the dock waiting for them were some of their employees. They wanted to see the boat and all the fish the men caught; they weren't disappointed.

When Paul got home he made some calls to friends and family. He planned a fish barbeque in his back yard, where as usual there would be beer and horseshoes.

He thought about his letter to Mary and after three days of watching the mailbox, her return letter finally came. His heart skipped a beat, and he took it straight to his room to read it.

Dearest Paul

    I read your letter; it was pleasing to hear from you, like a dream coming true. Years ago when Jim told my father why and what you did alone up the river we all knew we had all made a big mistake in thinking ill of you. I regretted my action and feeling towards you then. My life stopped at that time and now I feel it's starting up again. I knew I had lost you then and now I've been given a second chance
    Please be there for me. I don't think I could go through losing you again. I know our relationship was very demanding and we had great expectations as to the joy we would have being together. I want you badly. I feel that we should go slowly and make it happen. I would like to see you, I know the attraction will still be there, so lets plan for either you to come here or I go there or we could meet half way. In any case I'm anxious to be with you.

Love,
Mary

    Paul sat there holding the letter, looking off at the ceiling and thinking about her, wishing she were there with him now. He felt like jumping into his truck and going to her right this second.
    But what about Alice? Was it too soon? He loved her enough to make her his wife, but she was gone. Maybe Mary had been his true love all along. But where would they live? Winnipeg? California? As long as he was with her, he probably wouldn't care. Though there was also the question of having children. Mary was younger than he and could still have them, but what kind of father would he be?

The Innocent Beaver of Big Black River

He decided to answer the letter right away.

Dear Mary,

    Maybe we could meet halfway at Yellowstone National Park. I think you'd like it there. If you want, I can send you a bus ticket and we can meet, have a vacation and have each other to ourselves for a week.

                      Hope to see you soon,
                                    Paul

He got her letter back in a week and called the bus company to make the arrangements. He was excited. They were going to be together again, and this time they would be alone.

As he prepared his truck for the trip he remembered his trip with his Dad and it tickled the place in his heart for him. He called Mom and said he would be gone for a while. She was happy for him and wished him luck. Next he phoned the office and told Mark he would be going.

"No problem," Mark said. "I've got everything covered."

Paul left bright and early in the morning. As he drove he would look over at the passenger seat and imagined Dad was sitting there. Well, Dad, here we go again, Paul thought. I know you're here with me and we're traveling together again. He smiled.

After much concern that he would be late and miss Mary's bus, Paul finally arrived at Yellowstone. He pulled into the park and went to the office to get his cabin number and the location of the bus stop. He went to the cabin unpacked and set it up so it would be ready for Mary when she arrived. He looked at his watch. It was almost time. He drove over to the bus stop and parked there to wait. As he sat there he tried to plan what he would say when he first saw her. Out of the truck window he saw the bus arriving, so Paul got out of the truck and walked to the spot where the bus parked.

When the doors opened, Mary jumped out of the bus and right into his arms. They almost fell down, but Paul braced himself and hugged her. She was squealing and crying. She buried her face in his neck, and he carried her out of the way of the other passengers who were looking on with disbelief.

It had been five years since he last saw her. She had filled out a little but was still as beautiful as ever. His heart was pumping fast, and he was shaking with excitement. He had to find a place to sit down.

"Seeing you here now makes me know how much I really missed you."

"It's going to take me a long time to show you how much I missed you."

"You haven't changed. Maybe put on a few pounds, but I like you better that way." They realized that the passengers and passersby were watching them so they decided to get in the truck and head for the cabin.

Upon arriving at the cabin, Paul picked her up and put her on the bed; he crawled in beside her and they undressed, their bodies pressed tightly together. They had waited a long time for this and wanted to make the first time the best, they rolled and wrestled around until they were joined together pumping away, groaning and gasping and when it happened they pushed together, holding themselves there before rolling onto their backs, exhausted.

"I'd like to stay here the rest of the evening, but if we get up and shower, we can make it to the hotel to eat, then head over to the store and get some things so we can come back here and start all over again."

"Ok, but I shower first." Mary giggled and made a dash to get up and go into the shower.

"No fair, you got a head start."

The Innocent Beaver of Big Black River

They laughed as Paul entered the shower with her. They played with the water, washing each other's back. She reached down there and caressed him. Paul got out of the shower and dried off and put on his clothes as she did the same.

They drove to the hotel to eat, then went to the store, where they picked up some snacks and wine before heading back to the cabin. Paul unbuttoned her blouse and reached up to unhook her bra while she was working on his shirt. Eventually both were standing there in the nude looking at one another. They threw back the covers, and she pulled him down on top of her again.

"We have a lot of making up for lost time to do," she said. "So come on, lover, let's do it."

They made love over and over; he climaxed three times and she was getting wet and loose. Grabbing at one another it was hard for them to take a break, but they were learning as they progressed.

"Can you imagine what would have happened if we started this out there on the point running around in the snow in the nude, doing it over and over?" Paul asked as they lay in bed together. "I think we would've scared the wolves away instead of the other way around."

Paul said" Oh what a fool I've been. Such ecstasy. When I left Winnipeg the second time, I should have taken you with me, even if your family hated me."

"No, it was my fault. I let the others influence my decisions. After you left, my dad insisted that Jim tell us what you did back there in the woods. When he was done, we were all surprised, because no one had even thought of doing such a thing unless they wanted to commit suicide. We've always gone into the woods alone, but we were raised to know how to survive in there. When we heard what you had done we knew we had made a mistake about you. Me most of all."

"Let's not talk about the time that hurt us the most. We should just enjoy one another as long as we live. We have each other now, and that's what's important. I know now that you're good for me, and I hope it lasts forever."

Mary tickled his chest hairs again. "You have to quit first, Paul. You know I won't." She let out another giggle.

"I could spend the whole week in this cabin, but there are a lot of things to see, and I don't want you to miss them."

"What, are you ready to quit already?" She got up out of bed and ran from him. He chased her and grabbed her, and then they hugged and laughed some more.

"Seriously, we should pace ourselves," Paul said. "Or we may become sick from over-exertion."

"I know I won't wear out."

"What about getting pregnant?"

"I took care of that. We can talk about it later."

They dressed and went out for a walk. It was beautiful there in the park. Paul knew of the dangers there; having run into bears before, he kept a watchful eye for any movement. He and Mary walked hand-in-hand and he would put his arm around her and squeeze her.

With a chill coming on in the air, they meandered back toward the cabin. When they got back, Paul put some firewood in the stove and started it up. The smell of the wood burning made it cozy there, and the covers were already back, so they took of their clothes and got into bed and pulled the covers up and were soon asleep. In the middle of the night, Mary woke Paul up by handling him. She got on top and wiggled on him until he became aroused and she guided him into her. After they were done she went back to sleep.

The next morning they awoke early and lay there.

"Whenever you want me, just let me know."

"I already know that, thank you. And the same to you."

Paul knew that he had a permanent job to do for the rest of his life, and that's the way he wanted it. They were in each other's arms again, he tried to put it into her but she teased him, wiggling one way, then the other, until she gave in and let him inside her.

His eyes open wide, he came with a gush; it seemed like it would never stop. Over and over again he came, one orgasm after the other. She was doing it too and screaming with ecstasy. When they finished, they were exhausted.

"Now I feel like going back to sleep," he said.

"Oh no you don't. We're going out and see the sights before I miss them."

They drove around the park enjoying the sights and taking pictures. Even though she lived in the wild woods, she marveled at the beauty of Yellowstone with all its waterfalls, bubbling mud and geysers like Old Faithful. Paul told her about the pressure that built up under the earth's crust, much to Mary's amazement. She asked whether or not the whole park might explode, to which Paul laughed and kissed her on top of her head.

They picked up their lunch at one of the restaurants and continued on sightseeing. There was a bit of traffic but they were in no hurry. Soon they found themselves back at the cabin; they went in and both took showers but didn't bother to dress. They just lay there on the bed touching one another. Playing around, hugging and kissing, they joined in lovemaking. It seemed like they would never get tired or want to give it a rest.

She woke the next morning and cried, "Oh no, there's a man in my bed!"

"Yes, and guess what he's going to do."

Paul felt hungry but passed it off and started in again. They showered again. Paul liked having some one to wash his back.

"Rub harder."

They lathered one another down and then rinsed off, stepped out of the shower and dried one another.

"If you like we can go fishing today," Paul said to Mary. Her face lit up, and Paul, eager to please, took her to fisherman's bridge. All he had was line and small hooks.

"What are you going to fish with?" Mary asked.

"You'll see." He took her down a ways from the bridge, looking for his favorite spot. He found it, but it was fished out as most of the spots seemed to be. He came to a place that was impossible to fish because of a line of trees that bordered the lake and made it impossible to cast a line in the water.

"Mary, you wait right here next to the trees. I'll go into the trees and drop a line in the water. When I catch a fish I'll hand it out to you. You unhook it and hang it on that tree over there. When we have three of them we'll go back, ok?"

"You have a lot of faith in your ability to catch fish. As far as I know, we're still going to have to buy lunch." She laughed.

He crawled into the trees broke off a few branches to make an opening, taking out his line and hooks. He tied the hook to the line and dropped it into the water. It took only a few minutes when he had a nice fish on the line. He handed it out to Mary, who was delighted to take the fish and unhook it before handing the line back to Paul. When they caught two more, they walked down the road with their catch, heading for Paul's favorite restaurant. Once they got there, they walked back to the kitchen and knocked on the door. Harry, the head chef, answered. Paul was elated; he was still there after all these years. They hugged and danced around, thrilled by their reunion.

"I know just what to do with this," Harry said with a grin.

He took Paul's fish back through the kitchen door and gave instructions to his cooks. Then he came out to sit with Paul and Mary, and Paul explained that the third fish was a gift for him.

"Well, you did it again," Harry said. "Now you're going to have to tell them how you caught these fish. I know its just common sense, but they don't seam to have it."

"You know, I think you're right about that. I was walking along the lake, and I noticed that all the good holes were fished out. I had to go way down the side of the lake and find another place where it was hard to get at. If I tell them how to fish, the fish might just go extinct."

"Not all the spots are gone yet. Maybe I'll get a boat I can loan to you; then you'll be able to get to those spots by boat."

"You would do that for me?"

"I'm your friend, aren't I? Well that's what friends are for. Anyway, I could use a boat to go fishing when I have my time off."

"That's a deal," said Paul. "When I come through here again I'll stop in and get the boat."

"You'd better."

The fish arrived and they stopped talking and enjoyed their dinner. As usual, there was a group waiting outside the door to talk to Paul.

"I've only got a few minutes so listen closely and I'll tell you how I got these fish with just a hand line," he told them. After he was done he wished them luck and walked away with Mary.

They drove back to the cabin, where someone had come in and changed the sheets and left a chocolate kiss in the middle of the bed, which Mary ate before pushing Paul down onto the mattress.

It seamed the fish gave them extra energy. They pumped so hard, coming together and flopping over on their backs with fatigue. Paul lay there weakened and relieved. Mary got up and went to the bathroom.

"Do you have any more left? You had better eat some oysters and drink some eggnog or your well is going to run dry, and we don't want that." She laughed as he joined her in the bathroom. They both got in the shower.

"It's never been like this for me before and I'm sure enjoying it."

"My thoughts exactly. I've waited a long time and it sure was worth it."

"It's a good thing I resisted you at the point," Paul repeated. "Jim and Jean would have gone back to bed and stayed there."

"I had in my mind to go to the hunter's cabin in the woods where we would have had our privacy. We might still go out there some day." She winked at him.

"It took a lot for me to hold back. There were a lot of circumstances there that prevented us from doing what we wanted. Like your mother and father." He reached around her waist to lather her stomach. Mary saw the way the conversation was going and changed the subject.

"What are we going to do today?"

"First we eat, then we go and see the East and North ends of the park—just cruise around and take our time. How's that sound?"

"I don't care where we go I'm just happy to be with you. Did I tell you how much I love you this morning? I don't think I did." She ran into his arms hugging and kissing him. Looking right into his eyes said. "I love you."

They were drying off and getting dressed. Paul found himself getting excited again, and Mary could tell.

"Oh no, we're going out today and getting some fresh air," he said. He pulled her in close again. "And I love you, too."

"Come on, let's go." She found the rest of her clothes, grabbed her jacket and headed for the door. Paul was right behind her and felt her bottom as they went out.

There were a few sights they hadn't seen yet. He would guide her as they walked along so she wouldn't fall off the boardwalk paths, and when they stood at a wooden railing he stood behind her, pressing himself against her, holding her. She turned her head and looked at him asking with her eyes if he wanted to go back to the cabin. He looked at her with a silly grin.

"There are a couple more attractions we haven't seen, then we're through. Time to go."

"You mean that you want to leave after that? I'll miss our little cabin."

"I'll just have to make you another one."

"I'm still thinking of the hunters cabin in the woods back home. Just you and I and the birds and the bees. I don't want to share you with anyone."

They drove past two other sights but soon lost interest and decided to get something to eat. They stopped and got something to snack on and headed for the cabin. When they entered they thought it was a little cold, so Paul started a fire in the stove, put on his robe and sat in a lounge chair. He saw a little blue box sitting there on the table. He thought it must be something that Mary put there, so she wouldn't forget whatever she wanted to do with it. He took up the box and was looking at it. Mary approached and stood in front of him.

"Aren't you going to open it and see what's inside?"

"Am I supposed to?"

"If you like."

He opened the box, and there were the engagement and wedding rings he had bought for her five years ago. He took out the rings, took her hand and put the ring on her finger. She collapsed on him, crying like a baby. She was blubbering and trying to talk, but her words just wouldn't come out or make any sense. He reached up and took her in his arms and held her close. She tried to compose herself, but the more she tried the worse it got. He reached up and touched her nose, turning her face to him and kissing her. Looking at him she saw that he had tears in his eyes, too. Paul thought of how much she must have gone through in the years they'd spent apart.

They kissed and kissed again tasting the salt in each other's tears. Both started laughing at each other, which got them under control.

"I saved them knowing they would bring you back to me." She looked at the ring on her finger and started crying all over again. He held her close and started rocking her slowly.

By now, the cabin was nice and toasty. She stood, and he followed her, still wiping each other's tears and looking into one another's eyes. They knew that everything would be all right and started laughing again. They were both happy with each other and there joy was expressed with their laughter.

They reached out to one another holding hands, then touching one another like as if they couldn't believe what was happening to them.

They rubbed each other's backs and arms, pulled each other closer. Hands went to each other's private parts, tenderly massaging, pulling each other up close. They were shuddering with excitement. Their mouths locked together in one long kiss. They gently lowered each other down on the bed, robes falling to the floor. They lay there, continuing to massage one another. Teasingly, he pulled away. She tried to pull him back, but he resisted.

"What's the matter?" Mary asked. "Did I hurt you?"

"No, it's that when we do this, it brings back the memory of when we were at the point."

"Oh, you." Lightly, she started pounding on his chest. He took her back into his arms and they continued where they left off, only this time he pulled her on top of him. She was a little awkward, so he guided her. Her eyes lit up as she found all kinds of new feelings. Finally she collapsed, and as they hugged each other they fell asleep.

The next morning when they awoke, she was lying on top of him with her head on his chest. She was comfortable this way and didn't want to move. Her legs straddled his, and slowly she started to rub up against his hip. It felt good until she really got going. He didn't mind but he wasn't getting any, so he managed his legs in between her legs. She didn't have to steer him into her anymore; they knew each other's bodies by now. At first they went slowly and increased their speed a little at the time, until they were going full speed. In no time they reached a climax. She raised her head and kissed him.

"Good morning, sweetheart. What plans have you for me today?"

He couldn't answer because they were back in a firm kiss. Eventually he turned his face away from her, gasping for air.

"You said South would be fine with you. Still feel that way?"

"You know I do. You just want me to say it," she said, and made off like she was going to bite his nipple. He squirmed away

The Innocent Beaver of Big Black River

from her open mouth, which was trying to get the other one now. She moved her body so the one of her tits was over his mouth. He thought they were just the right size. The nipples weren't too big or too small, and when she got excited they stood up. He sucked on one, then with the tip of his tongue he tickled it. She sighed passionately and pulled away from.

"Remember that position so we can start there next time."

They packed up everything and loaded the truck. Paul drove to the office and signed out, paying his bill. They then went to have breakfast at the restaurant and say goodbye to Harry. After a few good words with Harry they were on their way. As they went along, Paul told Mary about his plans. They would travel to more sights like Bryce canyon, then to Zion canyon.

"Then on to Vegas to get married," he said. She threw herself at him. It was a good thing they were going slow. He pulled over, and she smothered him with kisses.

"You didn't say anything about Vegas."

"Well, we can't go on like this without being married, so we'll marry in Vegas. Then we can get married again in Winnipeg if you like.

"Could we? Oh, that would make me so happy."

"Then that's the plan."

Brice and Zion canyons impressed Mary, but when they entered Las Vegas she couldn't get over the lights.

"One night only," Paul said. Short honeymoon, I'm afraid."

He picked a chapel and pulled in. Mary had a nice dress, but it wasn't as nice as the one Paul had originally bought her. Nevertheless, she looked ravishing, and the wedding was nice; it made them feel that they would be together for the rest of their lives. Paul got a room at the Golden Nugget and got passes to two of the most popular shows, *La Parisian* and the *Follies Brazier*. When the girls were coming down in waves, she tried to cover Paul's eyes so he couldn't watch them.

When she saw all the beautiful girls parading around with nothing on she said, "They're beautiful, but how can they expose themselves like that?"

"They get paid a lot of money, and no one is allowed near them."

He stayed close to her when she played the slot machines.

"Aren't they afraid that someone will rob them with all this money lying around?"

"If the thief made it out of the casino he surely wouldn't make it out of town alive."

They left after two days instead of just one and headed for Kingman, Arizona. As they went through the Grand Canyon, Mary couldn't believe there could be such a big hole in the earth. They parked the truck and she edged toward the cliff, but Paul held her tight, not wanting to lose her now. When they were finished, they headed towards Los Angeles.

They stopped at a motel to satisfy their appetite.

"We're legit now, we can make all the love we want."

"Because we haven't been doing that already." Paul laughed. "Unless you've been holding out on me. You mean there's more?" At that they started wrestling on the bed and holding each other very tight. "I hope it never ends."

"Me too," Mary said.

CHAPTER SEVENTEEN

Paul called Erney's house and spoke to Mom.

"We're on our way and will be home in a few hours," he said. "Can you meet us there? After we get settled, we'll have the rest over."

"I'll leave right away so I can spruce up the house before you get there."

"Ok, Mom, I love you. See you soon."

They pulled into the driveway around five o'clock and were getting out of the truck when Mom came running up to them. She first grabbed Paul and hugged him, then held Mary. She had tears in her eyes.

"When I didn't hear from Paul, I knew you two were busy and I understood. I know you got married."

"You do?" Mary asked.

"You've both got rings on. And I couldn't be happier for you."

After bringing them inside, Mom pulled some things out of the fridge so she and Mary could make dinner.

"We got married in Vegas," Mary told her. Mom looked at Paul.

"You decided not to have a church wedding."

"We plan to have a church wedding at Barrens Landing," Paul said. "That should make it church legal."

"You are going to stay a while, aren't you? It wouldn't be right to just stop by and keep going. We want to get to know Mary and welcome her into the family properly."

The three enjoyed the evening, laughing and crying and telling each other that they had waited so long for this to happen.

"I just wish your father was here," Mom said. "After all, you never would have met if it weren't for him."

"But he is here, Mom. He's up there looking down and saying to me, 'Well, it's about time.'"

At this Mom smiled.

"We're planning to stay here about two or three weeks, Mom, so don't worry about us rushing out of here. I have some business to take care of and arrangements to make and like you said I would like Mary to meet the family. We should plan a get-together to welcome her."

Mom made the necessary phone calls. Everyone was excited to meet her. Paul called Mark and Jimmy, inviting them and getting a rundown on the business.

Paul and Mary were sitting in the living room while Mom fussed in the kitchen. Mary had helped her with the dishes, but Mom said not to worry about it; she and Paul should be alone. Mary returned to the couch.

"I've got it all figured out," Paul said to her. "We're going to see all the sights around here. That should keep you satisfied."

"Mom, I want to show Mary around Southern California," he said when Mom joined them. "You know, Disneyland, Knotts Berry Farm, Sea World, everything. So we'll be gone during the day, but we'll spend every evening with you. Is that ok?"

"That would be just fine."

Paul showed her the sights, and when Mom was away they made love at home; otherwise, they rented motels while traveling around. They agreed that they had to slow down, though, worrying that all the activity was a hazard to their health.

The Innocent Beaver of Big Black River

One day while Mary was out shopping with Mom, Paul met early with Mark and Jean at the office.

"I have some ideas about changes we can make to this business," Paul said. "First of all, no one will get paid by paycheck."

Mark and Jean looked at him in disbelief. He continued.

"Listen to the whole plan before you decide weather you think it will work or not. Since we've acquired a lot of property and businesses, I think we should use our assets as payment instead. If you need a car, we have all kinds to choose from; everything you'd need will be available to us. Like a barter system. All the employees can be a part of it. If you don't get paid, you don't have to pay an income tax. And we can use a point system, like timeshares do. That way if someone wants out we know how much to pay them.

"It's just a thought. As partners I would like you to think this over and include any thoughts you may have about it, and get back to me with your decision. We'll really have to do this right, with lawyers and everything, to make sure we don't make mistakes. Mark, I know you're busy, and I don't want to burden you, but I know you can handle it."

Paul read the smiles on Mark and Jean's faces. The idea just might work.

"If we do this, we'll need a lot of help. We have to pick people carefully. So think about our little meeting, write down any ideas, and we'll give ourselves a time frame so we won't drop the ball. Oh, and I think it's best if we keep this to ourselves until we're committed."

"Of course," Jean said.

"Any by the way, we're going to have a gathering at my house on Friday, and I'd like you both to be there."

They broke up the meeting and instead of shaking hands, both Mark and Jean gave Paul a big hug.

"Most successful people keep their wealth to themselves, but you want to share it with others," Mark said.

"You know what they say: one hand washes the other. And bring the kids Friday."

Paul went to meet Mary and Mom. They made him carry all the packages.

"Don't complain," Mary said. "Half this stuff is for you, anyway."

Paul, Mom and Mary went to get something to eat. Paul wasn't hungry, but he had coffee with them. He had the packages stacked up on the floor next to their table.

Jimmy walked up behind them. He touched Paul on the shoulder.

"Sit and have coffee with us, Jimmy. I was going to call you," Paul said. "Oh, I want you to meet Mary, my new bride."

"I heard you got married. Congratulations."

"I'm glad you came by. You can help me with their packages."

"You mean like I did in the old days."

"Speaking of which, how come you're not at the shop?"

"Took a break. I've got a good crew, so I can do that once in a while now."

Jimmy helped with the packages, even though he didn't have to.

"We're getting together Friday at the house, so bring the wife and kids so they can help you clean up the yard after." Jimmy and Paul laughed.

Arriving home, Paul carried the packages into the house. He let his wife and mother put them away. Mary came into the living room where Paul was sitting. She had on a dress that showed off her figure. Paul got up and came to her.

"What are you trying to do to me?" He whispered in her ear. "You know Mom's here. You should have gotten some jeans and a plaid shirt to hide your beautiful figure so as not to arouse me."

"Don't worry, I got some of those, too."

Friday arrived before they knew it. It was a casual affair. The men sat in a circle in the backyard and teased Paul.

"Does she have a sister?"

"How come you didn't tell us about her until now?"

Something was said about Indians and cousins. Paul gave them a look that put a stop to that line of conversation.

Mary was a hit with the girls in the house. She pitched right in, helping with the food. It was hard not to accept her into the family; she was joyful and laughed a lot, and they couldn't help but laugh with her.

Erney tried to get into a conversation with Mark about Paul's business.

"If you need any help, don't be afraid to ask. If I can't do the work myself, I can at least advise you when Paul isn't here."

Paul, who was talking to others, heard what Erney was saying and turned to Mark, smiling. When Mark looked at Paul, Erney knew that what he said didn't go over very well.

Everyone ate their fill, congratulating both Paul and Mary. There were a few gifts, mostly for Mary. When she opened them the group *ooh*ed and *aah*ed and made a big thing out of the gifts.

The party broke up with everyone hugging and kissing as they left.

"Glad you could make it, Mark," Paul said. "Now they know that you're one of us, I'm going up North again for a while. I'm happy I made the choice I did. Now I won't worry while I'm gone. I'll keep in touch with you by phone when I can. Work on what we talked about so we can be prepared to act when we're ready."

The next few days Paul got his things together. The boat would come in handy again. He liked pushing it going up to the river. He figured out what he could take in the boat without overloading it. Jimmy came and checked it out so Paul wouldn't have any problem. He thanked Jimmy for not saying anything about Alice in front of Mary, and Jimmy wished him a good trip. Arrangements were made with Erney about Mom's care.

In the morning, they were on their way. After getting used to the road again, Mary sat looking straight ahead.

"What's wrong, dear?"

"I feel like I'm living in a dream and don't want to wake up. My life is beyond expectations thanks to you."

"After I get through with you tonight, you'll know it's not a dream."

"I was hoping you would say that." Snuggling up to him, she gave him a squeeze.

"Not now. I said tonight, and we've got a long way to go."

"Are we going through Yellowstone again?

"No I was thinking of traveling up the coast on Route 101 so you can see the ocean all the way. First we'll go through the Sequoias so you can see the giant redwood trees, continuing north to Queen Victoria Island so you can see the pretty flowers, then cut back through Banff and Jasper National Parks. The scenery is beautiful all the way and we may see some game in the road,"

She took out her Manitoba map and opened it up.

"We could take Route One to Winnipeg and unless we want to see Pete and Rose we could take Route Six North to Grand Rapids, cross the lake to Popular River, where my mother is. I was hoping you'd say we were going back to our little cabin in Yellowstone, but we can go to the hunters cabin at Big Black River instead and stay as long as we like."

"You really like the hunters cabin? What is it about that place that's so special to you?"

"All the Indian girls that get married go there on their honeymoon. It's superstition that if you go there on your honeymoon, your marriage will be a success. I know our marriage will be a success for as long as we live, Paul."

"If that's what you want to do, fine by me."

When they got to Grand Rapids Mary directed him to a friend who had a general store with a large fenced parking lot for people who needed a place to keep their cars while they were on the lake.

The owner was glad to see Mary and asked about her brothers. When they were done talking, he turned to Paul.

"I heard about you. They call you the wolf exterminator. You're either good or lucky, but I'm guessing you're good. So don't worry about your rig. We take care of our own here and now you're part of us. There's a good spot between the buildings back there. We have a large tarp to cover your truck and trailer. We tie the dog up when we go out there and release him after. He knows what to do."

He thanked the storeowner, and they were on their way across the lake. It felt good to be at the controls of his boat again. He set his cruise control and let her go by herself, then went back and sat with Mary.

"I was watching you set up your controls. You really like this boat, don't you, Paul?"

"It was made to my specifications. There's no other like it."

She went to the controls, not liking that the boat went along by itself with no guidance from anyone. He followed her and unlocked the steering, but when she turned the wheel the least bit and found it very sensitive, so she left it alone. They sat side by side, whizzing along on top of the water. He put his arm around her, and they both smiled and then laughed. She realized that she, like his boat, was now a part of him.

She gave him directions to landmarks on the shore where they were going. Her directions were right on and they went straight into the landing where they wanted to tie up. Evidently the noise of the motor and the speed and rooster tail attracted someone at the dock, who called others.

"Here they come."

A group was waiting at the shore to help them tie up their boat and give them hugs. Nothing was said about the past experiences Paul had there. They were all glad he was back with them again and that Mary at long last had her dreams fulfilled. Her mother came to her with tears in her eyes as she embraced her daughter.

"Now I know you're happy, and I'm happy for you. May you be happy the rest of your life, and may you give me some grandchildren." She laughed.

They walked to Mary's mother's house, which is where they were going to stay while they were in Popular River.

Word got around real quick that there was going to be a wedding and reception there. The priest was called and arrangements were made. It seemed like everyone who'd heard about it would be there; the wedding had to be held outside to accommodate them all. They both wore suits, and everyone agreed they made a beautiful couple.

There was plenty of food and drink at the reception. Everyone ate and drank their fill. Congratulations were granted and toasts were made and eventually every one went home. Jim, Paul and Mary sat around Mary's mother's cabin and drank coffee to sober up. Mary said she and Paul were going to the hunters cabin for their honeymoon.

"I don't think there's much there now," Jim said. Paul looked at Mary to see if she changed her mind.

"I don't care. We can go if only to spend a night in our sleeping bags," Mary said.

"At the landing there's a place where you can tie up your boat, but there's no one there to watch it. It should be fine, but you can never tell."

Preparations were made in the morning. They tied one of Jim's canoes behind Paul's boat and headed out. They couldn't go too fast or they would have filled up Jim's canoe with water. When they got to the landing, they noticed the buildings were rotting with no one to care for them. Mary felt a little sad at the condition of it. This is where she was raised.

They took the canoe and paddled together. Mary burst out laughing.

"What's so funny, Mary?"

"I was just remembering when you left here on your way upriver by yourself. Remember the trouble you had with the canoe? You almost ended up out in the lake."

They paddled along enjoying the scenery, noticing how things changed over the years. They came to the waterfalls and pulled up to the landing where Mary helped to carry their supplies up to the top. Paul wanted to show her how he could carry the canoe by himself, but she grabbed her end and made it easy for him. They loaded the canoe again and continued up the river. They came to the landing where the path led to the cabin and beached the canoe.

The first things they carried to the cabin were the thirty-thirty rifle Jim insisted they take and Dad's shotgun.

"Why don't you stay here at the cabin," Paul said. "I'll carry the stuff up."

He didn't like the condition of the cabin. The wood was rotten, the windows were broken out, and the door was hanging by leather straps. The inside was filthy. Animals had been having a good time playing in there.

"We'll just push the mess out of the way. It's only for one night," Mary said.

He headed back to the canoe for another load, and when he returned he needed to relieve himself, so he went to the outhouse, which was a short distance from the cabin.

"That outhouse doesn't look too good. If I get stuck in there you'll have to come and get me out."

He went in, dropped his pants and sat down. The boards were rotten so he couldn't put much pressure on them or he would fall in the hole below.

He was just about finished when they attacked. He had pulled up his pants and was tightening his belt when one hit the outhouse from the back, knocking it forward with the door down so Paul couldn't get out. At first Paul didn't know what happened. Then he heard the growling. Mary was out there by herself, Paul thought. She needs my help. He kicked the side of the house and broke the boards away, so as to make a hole big enough to crawl through.

A wolf was waiting for him. The only weapon he had was his knife. He always carried it with him now that he was up. It had saved him more than once before.

He heard shots. Mary must be shooting at them. He went out feet first, kicking as he went. He didn't get a chance to stand up. The wolf was on top of him. He held his left arm in front of his throat and with his right he brought up the knife and slit the wolf's belly wide open, guts spilling out as the animal went limp.

Paul looked over at Mary. There were two of them after her. She shot one, and the other left her alone to lunge at Paul. It jumped but Mary shot again and it fell. Paul went to her. She was a mess. Her face had been bitten and the flesh hung from her cheeks. Paul grabbed a cloth from their bags and pulled her back against the cabin to prop her up. He sat for a few minutes to catch his breath, then removed the cloth from Mary's face to see how bad it was. The wolf bit into her forehead with its upper teeth and sunk its lower teeth into her jawbone. He put the cloth back to keep the wound clean.

They were both sitting there when out of the woods came Jim. Mary looked the worst so he took care of her. Joseph appeared behind Jim; evidently they knew the condition of the cabin and had come to fix it up for Paul and Mary. Jim picked up Mary and headed for the canoe; she had lost a lot of blood and needed medical care. Joseph and Paul collected their belongings, which were now scattered. Paul's left arm was a mess. He was lucky the bite didn't damage the bone. They made their way down the river as fast as they could. At the falls they left one canoe and all the supplies and piled into the other. They got down to the landing as fast as they could, uncovered Paul's boat and raced at full speed down to Selkirk so they could get Mary to the hospital.

At the hospital they got her stable and got a plastic surgeon to sew her up. He said he did the best he could, that she would need a lot of work done to correct the damage done to her face. When she came out of surgery, she was a little groggy and didn't talk much, so they put her in recovery. Paul got his arm sewed up, too. He would need additional work done, but there was nothing to worry about. He would be all right.

When Mary came out of recovery Paul was there with his arm bandaged up. She looked at him with a tear in her good eye.

"I'm sorry, I'm really sorry. If I hadn't insisted on going to the cabin this never would have happened. What are we going to do now?" She insisted on them bringing in a mirror and when she saw her face she let out a scream. "My life is over," she cried. "I never want to be seen in public again."

She wanted to go to the hunters cabin to live. It would be isolated, she told him, and no one could cringe at the sight of her.

He started making preparations for the things he would need: lumber, windows, doors, hardware, shingles. Jim and Joseph helped. He called down to Mark and told him what happened. Mark took down a list of Paul's requests and had all the necessary items transported out to him on a truck.

Paul found an Indian who could operate the tractor he'd procured from Mark and instructed the man to build a road from the factory to the hunters cabin. A sled was made for the tractor to pull, and all the big stuff would be hauled in that way. When the road was done, they got to work on a landing strip and a radio tower, then a series of smaller cabins. Paul even bought himself a little plane called a beaver and hired a pilot to fly it.

Mary was happy with the arrangements. Jim found a couple and got them to come out and stay in one of the cabins in exchange for work. Their names were Ruth and John. Ruth worked in the house for Mary while John did handiwork for Paul and acted as security guard.

When the lodge was completed Jim and Joseph came out and they had a celebration at the main cabin. Mary's mother was with them. They tried to get her to come and stay with Mary, but she declined, saying she was with her people and liked it that way. Paul raised his glass.

"I want to thank you all for all the help you gave us. This turned out to be a nice place, and we have the wolves to thank for it."

"So what exactly happened on the honeymoon?" Jim asked.

"We were moving our supplies up here and Paul had to go to the outhouse. Everything was peaceful and quiet until they came out of the woods and ran towards the outhouse. I picked up the rifle and started shooting. I got one of them. Another one came at me as I was shooting. Then one started after Paul and I guess I shot it."

"How could you shoot in the condition you were in? How could you see?" Paul asked.

"I don't know. All I do know is that I didn't want them hurting you."

"You know, that's the second time now that you've saved me," Paul said.

CHAPTER EIGHTEEN

Paul ran a phone line all the way from Barrens Landing so he could keep in touch with the business in California. Mark gave him a rundown as to what was happening and how the plan for the new business model was going. They had a few employees who went for it. They bought more businesses not only to make money but also to allow them to furnish their employees with what they needed. They bought a large condominium complex so they had a place where all the employees lived. They also bought out the shopping center nearby. The owner was glad to sell. He didn't know of The Pocket Management Company but that was all right; he got a cash deal.

At the Pocket Management Company a Mr. Bently approached their receptionist and asked for Mr. Morgan. He had an appointment. She checked to see if Mark was busy and was told to show him in.

"Hello, Mark. I'm Mr. Richard Bently of The National News Service." He shook his hand. "You can call me Dick."

"Pleased to meet you. What can we here at Pocket Management do for you?"

"I'm following up on a story about your company, and I'm here to get the facts straight. According to what I've learned so far, your company is very profitable. But they say that you don't pay your employees a salary. How do you keep them and how do you encourage them to do a good job for you?"

"Actually its simple and its no secret. We use a kind of timeshare method. I don't have the time right now to go into detail, but if you want a job, we could fit you in. You'd like it here. All our employees do. I'll tell you what, why don't we meet for lunch at the park?"

Dick looked a little disappointed. He had other things to do and figured this would take only a few minutes. Now he was getting involved. But he needed the story, so he agreed.

At the park, Dick found Mark sitting on a bench waiting for him. As he approached, Mark stood and guided him to a hotdog vender.

"Hey, Pete. The usual. And one for my friend here."

The hotdog vendor gave one to Dick, and Mark started walking away.

"We haven't paid," Dick said.

"That's part of our system. Our employees don't pay, the company does. I asked you to join me because this is the best way to explain how our business works."

"Who's running all this, anyway? Seems no one's seen the guy. Does he even exist?"

"The owner is Mr. Paul Paquette, The reason for the name Pocket Management. He started this business and I became his partner. He's away and I don't know when he'll be back. We communicate once a month now and he's satisfied with that; it's a simple business to run. Everyone is more or less their own boss."

"I would like to know more about Mr. Paquette."

"Can't say anything else about him unless I've got his permission."

"Mr. Paquette is a peculiar person. Very wealthy with a thriving business and he's nowhere to be found."

"He's the nicest person you could ever meet. He's helped more people than you can count, and he's still helping people."

They were making their way out of the park. As the men were about to depart in their separate directions, they shook hands once more.

"I know the paper's going to want a follow-up on this. My boss is going to want me to meet with Mr. Pauquette. Can you arrange it?"

"I'll do my best."

After a series of phone calls back and forth, it was finally agreed that Dick might be able to go meet Paul up in Manitoba if he so desired. It was set up for him to fly to Winnipeg, rent a car, and drive up the west side of the lake to a general store where he would leave it. He would be met and transported by boat to meet Mr. Pauquette.

"You must be Dick," a man said to him when he pulled into the store's lot.

"That's me. And you are?"

"Jim. Come this way."

Jim put the boat up on plane and they were on their way. The wind blew his hat off into the water. Jim spun the boat around and picked it up, putting in his lap.

They arrived at the landing and walked down the new road to the clearing. Jim carried his rifle, which was all right with Dick. They came to a grassy clearing with a nice large cabin and three smaller cabins and headed for the former. Jim knocked on the door, and Paul answered.

"Did you have a good trip?"

"My heart's been beating out of my chest since I got here. I'm having a grand time and getting paid for it to boot. If you won't tell my boss I won't."

The cabin was fairly large. Who ever built it did a professional job. Some one moved in the other room but didn't come out.

"So that we can feel at ease, I would like to know why you came all this way to ask me about my business."

"There are stories going around about another Howard Hughes building a mega business. They don't know where he lives or why he keeps to himself in seclusion. Naturally when there are fortunes at stake there are a lot of interested parties. A lot of interested parties would like to talk to you. Some of them doing business with your company which has the highest ratings. The main question is, how can you run a business as large as it is without being there?"

He looked at Paul for some answers, but got none.

"Would you like some coffee?"

Dick thought for a moment he got the put-off treatment. He had laid his cards on the table, and now it was up to Paul.

"Sure, coffee would be good right now."

Jim just sat there watching and listening. Paul went to the kitchen. Jim glanced at him, and Paul motioned for him to come to him.

"Can you stick around for a while?" Paul asked Jim. "I don't know if want to go along with what he wants. I need a little time to think this over."

"I have some important things to take care of, so I can't stay all night. Maybe we could eat and talk about other things. If you haven't made up your mind by then, you could keep him here for a day or so. Then I can come back and take him out to his car. Hey, what about Mary? Did she know he was coming?"

"That's part of why I agreed to have him here. I told her he was coming, that it was about my business. I am hoping she will get used to the idea of having company. We just have to go slow with her."

Paul carried the hot coffee back to the sitting area and gave some to Dick.

"I haven't yet made up my mind about putting my life out there for the whole world to criticize. I need a day or two to think it over, if that's all right with you. Jim's going to be leaving soon, so you can go with him tonight, or you can stick it out and see if I give you the story."

Dick's face fell.

"I thought that we had already agreed to the idea that I was to get your story. Otherwise my boss wouldn't have allowed me to come. I've traveled a long way. I don't want to go back empty-handed."

"Okay, then, suit yourself. You can sleep in one of the little cabins, and you'll take your meals in the big cabin with us. Thing is, there are some rules you have to follow. See, my wife is badly disfigured and very shy about it. She'll probably stay out of your sight while you're here, but I would appreciate your cooperation in respecting her space and wishes. She comes first in everything I do. At a moment's notice I may ask you to leave, and I expect you to understand."

Dick did not expect anything like this. He looked at Paul and Jim with bewilderment.

"Well, your wish is my command. Just let me know what you want done and how you want me to act."

"She hasn't been around anyone new since the accident, so I don't know. I guess we'll have go slowly and see what happens. Let's go sit and eat."

As they sat Dick saw that Henry and his wife were already there. They shook hands and took their places at the table. The food smelled good, and Dick was hungry. Paul noticed that another place had been set but made no mention of it. They were about to start passing the serving bowls around when Mary appeared in one of the bedroom doorways. She was dressed nice and stood there waiting to be recognized.

She had an embroidered handkerchief fashioned over the right side of her face. She used hairpins to hold it in place. Curiosity must have gotten the best of her in regard to their guest.

"Are you going to introduce us?" Mary's voice sounded mostly discernible, like someone speaking with their tongue in their cheek.

"Yes, dear. This is Mr. Dick Bently of the Union News Agency. Mr. Bently, this is my wife, Mary. Dick is here to find out why I'm up here and not down in California where my business is."

As Paul spoke he walked to Mary, put his arm around her and guided her to her place at the table. She was seated next to Jim, who sat next to Dick. Dick said he liked the moose meat that had been prepared and complimented the smell of the wood cabin.

The conversation was just loud enough to draw attention away from the way Mary ate; she sucked and slurped her food, covering her mouth with her hand. Paul was proud of her and squeezed her hand and smiled his approval. She smiled back with her good eye, as if to say, "See, I can do it."

After dessert, Dick thanked Paul and everyone else before being shown to his cabin. It was clean, and to his surprise it had hot running water. He noticed that Paul and Henry were sitting outside smoking their pipes. So he walked over.

"Can I join you?"

"Sure, have a seat," Paul said.

"I have a million questions, so many my head is spinning. I want to ask you everything, I don't to forget one single detail."

"Hang on a minute," Paul said. "Let's figure out what it is we're doing here."

"What do you mean? I thought we were doing an interview."

"That's just it. I don't want that. You take my words and twist them around to make a good story to sell your papers. No, what I want is for you to write my biography word for word in book form. It gets copyrighted and your company gets to use statements in the book for their paper. We share in the proceeds. If someone wants to read my story, they can pay me for it. This way they can't change what I've said. If that is agreeable, lets get started."

"Now I know how you made such a successful business: you're a hard bargainer. Why don't we get started first thing tomorrow?"

"We have another problem."

"What's that?"

"Timber wolves. You saw my face and my arms. And my wife. That's why we're out in the middle of nowhere. You have to be very careful around here. They can attack without notice, so don't go anywhere alone. Can you shoot?"

"I haven't had much practice, but I was a sharpshooter in the service."

"Well, we don't need you to shoot people. Just wolves."

"Sounds ok to me. And I'm not going to be a pest while I'm around. I'm here to do some writing. I don't plan to do any wandering, especially not now that I know what's out there. Though I would like to see one of these wolves from a distance. Maybe take a picture." He looked out the window at the darkening sky. "Now I know what your people are saying about you is true. I can only imagine what's going to be in this book."

"Get a good night's rest, 'cause you're going to need it."

For breakfast they had bear sausage, homemade bread, eggs and lots of coffee. Dick nonchalantly reached for seconds and smiled. Mary had her handkerchief on but it seemed to get in the way. After breakfast Paul and Dick relaxed in the family room. Dick laid out his equipment on the coffee table.

"I'm going to say something, and if I'm out of line I'll drop it," Dick said. "I have a close friend in Hollywood. He's the best plastic surgeon there is. People come from all over the world for his services. I'll give you his card, and you don't have to mention my name. He'll know I'm the one who sent you, because I send him the worst ones. A lot of his clients are Hollywood stars, and once a year he travels around the world helping poor children. I can take Mary's picture with the newspaper's camera and give it to him, see what he can do."

"We tried that and didn't get a good response. She is very sensitive about her face and doesn't want anyone to see her."

"Ok, forget it, then," Dick said. "We'll get down to why I'm here. So I'm going to sit and listen to your story with the recorder. If I'm confused I'll ask questions." He pushed some buttons. "Go ahead, you're on."

Paul started from the beginning and tried to make it as perfect as possible. He emphasized his good friends, how without them he couldn't have achieved his success. There were times when Dick couldn't believe what Paul was telling him. Paul went into the bedroom and brought out some pictures of the wolves they had shot, the police report of Alice's drowning, photos of Dad and Mark and Jean.

They recorded for two days until Paul was satisfied that he included all the things he wanted in the book. He kept a copy of the recording and said he didn't want the book printed until he approved of it. So Dick agreed to send a copy to him for his approval.

On the third day, Jim came back for Dick and took him to his car. They shook hands and were looking forward to seeing each other again sometime. When Jim returned, he and Paul say and talked about the visit. As Jim and Paul were chitchatting, Mary came and sat next to Paul.

"How did I do with my first guest?" she asked.

"Seems like you're adjusting to the idea that you're going to have people coming here. Have you given any more thought to having plastic surgery done?"

Mary shrugged.

"Dick seems to think his doctor is the best," Paul said. "We could give it a try, send him some of your pictures and see what he says. Dick gave me a piece of paper with the name on it."

"I know how you feel about your business. Even though you have Mark there, you'd like to be there yourself. Our way of life here keeps you away from your way of life there," she said. "So lets take some pictures and see what happens."

Clear pictures were taken showing her face up close. Paul sent them to Doctor Moscowitz, and three weeks later they received a package from the doctor with before and after photos of his patients and a letter explaining the procedure. Some of the people looked pretty bad before he performed the surgery. Paul and Mary agreed that they should try one more time, so Paul contacted the doctor's office and made an appointment for her. He also called his pilot and made arrangements for transportation to Hollywood.

At the doctor's office, Mary wore a makeshift veil made from her crocheted handkerchief. The doctor stood in front of her. He slowly removed her veil and touched her face lifting it so he could see all the damage. She jerked and closed her eyes.

"Don't worry, we're just getting acquainted, your face and me. It will be mine for the next month. And when I get through, I will give it back to you brand new. Let's get started."

Paul and Mary looked at each other.

"We were thinking this would be an evaluation. We wanted to think it over," Paul said.

"You've had a long time to think it over. I've already made arrangements, and we're admitting you to the hospital right away. There's a bed all made up for you and everything."

"You're my kind of guy," Paul said. "Let's get it done."

As the weeks went by, Mary ended up with lots of bandages on her face. Between operations she convalesced at a resort that was used exclusively for patient recovery. She was isolated from the scrutiny of strangers, and she was happy with this procedure. Paul was satisfied, too. After the operation she went back to her old self again. Mary was laughing and smiling, beautiful as ever.

"You're as beautiful as you ever were. I'm going to have to keep my eye on you so I don't lose you." Paul had tears in his eyes.

"You don't have to worry. You're the only one for me."

She was released, and they went to Paul's condo where they spent the night together for the first time since the surgery. Paul still had the houses in Riverside, but they were rented, and he was through with staying at his parents' old place.

Mark and Jean called wanting to celebrate Mary's successful operation. They had picked out a fancy restaurant and reserved a table by the window.

As they lifted their glasses and made a toast, Mary said she had something to add.

"After the final bandages were removed the doctor took pictures of the results and being very well pleased sent the best copies to some studios he knew well. Usually he just does it for advertizing but this time he got back a response."

"And?" Jean asked.

"And if it's all right with you, Paul, I'm scheduled for a screen test."

Everyone at the table stood and clapped. Paul kissed her.

"If that's what you want, go for it."

Mark cleared his throat.

"Oh, and I made some calls about a place to stay for you guys. Knowing how you'd like to be close to the water, I found a beautiful home in Huntington Beach harbor. It has a dock in the backyard for your boat, and I really think you'll like it."

Paul gave Mark a questioning look. Mark continued.

"Don't worry, you trained me well. I got it at a good price. The owner had a stroke and the wife was very cooperative when it came to paying in cash."

"How lucky are we to have you, Mark," Paul said.

It turned out Mark had already furnished the harbor house using some of the antique sailing paraphernalia. All Paul and Mary had to do was make themselves comfortable.

After they were settled, Paul called Jim. Mary's eyes lit up. She wanted Jim to see how good she looked. Jim asked if he could come down for a vacation with his truck and boat since they'd just gotten two new river cruisers. It took two days for Jim to make the trip and was tired when he arrived.

Paul helped him drive the rig to the boat ramp, then to the dock. Jim was impressed when he saw the cruiser parked there. They visited on the patio, looking at all the boats. Paul's gaze drifted to Jim and Mary.

"I left here seven years ago with my dad to see you, and now I'm back here again. A lot has happened since," Paul said. "But I wouldn't change a thing."